THE CAPTIVE

A CONTEMPORARY REVERSE HAREM ROMANCE
(SAVAGE MOUNTAIN MEN)

MIKA LANE

GET A FREE SHORT STORY!

Get a free short story!
Join my Insider Group

Exclusive access to private release specials, giveaways, the opportunity to receive advance reader copies (ARCs), and other random musings.

ISBN ebook 978-1-948369-26-8
ISBN print 978-1-948369-27-5

Like deals and other cool stuff?
Sign up for my newsletter!

CHAPTER 1

JOELLE

I'd thought Vegas was the place to disappear. Get lost. Never be found.

With its endless cacophony of taxi horns, slot machines, barkers announcing buffets, half-price show tickets, cheap alcohol, and cheesy bachelorette parties, I was shrouded—in a good way. I'd wanted to disappear—just melt into the sea of humanity. Become anonymous.

I'd never stand out in the shitshow that was Vegas.

Nor did I want to. For good reason.

But now, on Savage Mountain, I realized I'd one-upped Vegas. Not in the excitement category, although that depended on how you felt about nature and the great outdoors. No, *this* was the place to run away to, I was quickly learning. There wasn't another soul for miles. It would take a goddamn drone or NASA satellite and a research team to find me here.

I looked up in the sky. You never knew, even if you couldn't see it.

Satisfied that technology wasn't after me that particular day, I floated lazily on my back in the shallow stream just next to the tent I'd successfully, and impressively pitched. I probably wouldn't have gone in the water—beyond just soaking my feet—had it been deeper than, say, my thighs. But it was as if nature had given me my own perfect little personal wading pool. The rocks on the bottom were bumpy and a little painful to feet that hadn't gone barefoot in years, but as soon as I was in deep enough I launched myself, suspended, weightless, and watching shots of sun bust through the overhead trees like a moth-eaten canopy.

Almost made me believe there was a god.

My hair floated around my head in that way hair does in water, where you can pretend to be a mermaid or if you're feeling more cynical, Medusa. I wasn't quite sure which I felt like that day. Maybe both.

A couple floaty bugs alighted on the surface of the water, and took off again just as quickly.

Were they eating? Drinking? Mating? When bugs got down to it, did they do it like mammals, or more like fish, or just some sort of drive-by spawning?

Should have brought some kind of nature book.

My tits bobbed in the water as I drifted, nipples tight like little beads as I shimmied to see how much the girls would sway. Beyond my non-mountains of flesh—who was I fooling, my little tits had never bounced and probably never would—was the belly button piercing I'd gotten back when all my girlfriends were doing it. I'd been a big enough idiot to follow them. And beyond that was the small patch of hair I let grow above the area I'd had permanently lasered. Yes, I'd subjected my entire crotch to laser hair removal. Another of my dumbass ideas.

At the time it seemed sexy, and I guessed it still was. I mean, guys liked it, sure. Christ if you had hair on your pussy these days, guys would go running like you had goddamn herpes or something. In fact, I think a guy would rather fuck a girl with herpes than one with freaking pubic hair.

How messed up was that?

But as time passed after my stupid laser treatments, it dawned on me that someday I would be an *old lady with no pussy hair*. And that would not be hot. Not at all.

At least the non-sagging tits would be nice, kind of. Better than the sagging softballs of silicone some of my friends had, sure that implants would be just the thing to get them where they wanted to go.

I'd made some fucked up choices for sure, many of them far worse than a pierced belly button and a permanently bald pussy. But I was grateful I'd not gone too overboard with the tattoo thing. My friend Pippa had, and now she had to cover up all the time. I'd kept mine somewhat discreet. Maybe not the hippest decision, but I'd saved some money and a little bit of hassle.

I'd made some good life decisions, too, if I thought about it, although they seemed few and far between most days. But on that particular day, I was happy as hell to be camping—yes, *me*, camping—in the middle of nowhere, alone. Floating in a stream. Butt naked, soaking up the rays.

Yes, I was camping alone. Tell anyone I knew and they'd tell you to shut the fuck up. *Jo, camping?* Um, don't think so. The closest I'd ever come to camping would have been a weekend at the Mirage, or maybe the Bellagio if I'd done well that week at my waitressing job.

Sad truth was, I never did that well. So in reality, I never stayed at the Mirage or Bellagio.

Yet here I was.

Pippa was supposed to be with me. Pippa, my best friend and coworker at the shithole titty bar Maid to Order. Cute name, brought tourists and locals alike from all over Vegas. The restaurant even had ads on the backseats of cabs, and doormen handed out cards with ten percent off your first drink—that's how classy a joint we were.

I fluttered my arms around the water just enough to move closer to the embankment where I'd gotten into the stream. When I found a rock big enough to support my bum, I sat, pulling my legs up under me and pressed a finger into my opposite forearm to see if I was getting too much sun. It left a white spot surrounded by red.

Yup, time to get my bare ass out of the water and

into the shade. I hated to leave the baking sensation that warmed my skin and relaxed me so completely. But a pasty girl like me would be in misery all fried to a sunburned crisp.

Time to cover up.

I moved my towel under a shady tree—seriously, did I mention it was like someone had created a perfect, custom-made campsite, just for me?—and lay down with my book. But instead of reading, I flipped onto my back and watched the water bead up before completely evaporating from my skin.

Skinny dipping was glorious. Why didn't I do it more often?

Pippa and I had arranged a few days off together from Maid to Order, something our boss protested like we were pulling out her fingernails. She was seriously a bitch just to be a bitch. But we'd pressured her and she'd caved even though we knew she'd make us pay later by assigning us lousy shifts, or giving us tables with the creepiest dudes. But I could handle that shit. I had before and lived to tell about it.

Plus, we had an important reason for taking time off and leaving town. A very good reason.

It had been Pippa's brilliant idea to camp. Supposedly she and her hippy parents had gone all the time when she was a kid, and she'd always proclaimed herself a camping expert. Never mind that she'd barely been outside of Las Vegas since she'd arrived at eighteen years old.

She'd gone out and borrowed a shitload of camping equipment, and purchased the rest—of course hitting me up to cover half the cost. With all the stuff she'd collected, you'd have thought we were climbing goddamn Mount Everest. I mean, what was the point of camping if you had to take every freaking gadget ever invented to make the experience more comfortable? You might as well stay at home, if you asked me.

But Pippa didn't ask me, so I kept my mouth shut.

I wasn't going to rain on the parade of the best friend I'd ever had. Seriously, the girl had been nothing but supportive since the I'd met her—starting on my first day at Maid to Order—when the other girls were giving me death stares and sleazebag customers furtively fondled my ass as I walked by. Instead of being a mean girl like the other waitresses, she'd taken me aside and told me that as miserable as it was to walk around the "breastaraunt" half-naked in a flimsy little maid's uniform, the tips were out of this world. Suck it up for a couple years, she'd told me, and then you'd be on easy street. At least, that was *her* plan.

And so it became my plan. Why not? It wasn't like I had anything better to do.

No, at that moment, life had little in store for me. But I had a future. I knew it. I was a songwriter, and was saving to get a demo tape made. But I needed some serious cash for that, not to mention connections. So, I kept sucking it up at Maid's, miserable though the place made me.

But two days before our Savage Mountain trip, after we'd practiced pitching our tent in my living room, testing the camp stove on my balcony, and schlepping around in our hiking boots to break them in, Pippa slammed her finger in the goddamn cash register at work. I am not kidding.

I wish I were joking, but one look at her purple finger, swollen fatter than a sausage, kept me from being too pissed. The poor girl really was in agony, and in fact, the doctor said she'd probably lose her fingernail if he didn't drain the blood. So camping was out. For her, that was. She took her vacation days and headed to L.A., where there would be no tents, sleeping bags, or outdoor cooking.

The girls at work, who'd warmed up to me after their initial hazing, told me I should go anyway. That I knew what I was doing, and that I'd probably be fine.

Probably. Thanks, girls.

So I'd decided *what the hell.* I'd driven three hours north, and two hours in some other direction—I still wasn't sure which—and ended up at the very trailhead we'd mapped out and planned on for weeks. Thank god for GPS.

It was clear when I'd arrived at the right place, in part because there was nowhere else to go. The road abruptly ended, and on one side of it was just enough room for a couple cars to park. I pulled over as far as I could just in case someone actually did come along, and grabbed my hulking pack off the passenger seat. I got it up on my shoulders without wrenching my back, just as I'd practiced, and tightened the padded belt around my waist. I only had a couple miles to hike to the campground, but I wanted to do it the right way. Besides, when was the last time I walked anywhere with forty pounds on my back?

How 'bout never?

I'd pressed *lock* on my key fob, and zipped it into my shorts pocket for safekeeping. And that was *all* I did.

I must have stood by my car for an hour trying to screw up the courage to set foot on the trail that loomed before me. It was pretty enough, and there was nothing intimidating about it, if you didn't have a wild, sick imagination like I did. What if I got lost? What if I saw Bigfoot? Or a squirrel?

I mean, I'd seen plenty of crappy movies about young women who go off into the wilderness. Who the hell did I think I was, going camping *by myself*?

Fucking idiot, I was.

But I eventually put one foot in front of the other, making slow but steady progress, my still-stiff hiking boots padding softly on the pine needle-lined trail. In less than an hour on the trail, I'd reached a well-marked clearing. It was *the* campsite that Pippa and I had chosen from our trail maps. There was an obvious flat spot to put up my tent, a place where I could cook, and even better—where I might take a swim.

Like I'd said, the place was freaking *made for me*. I

8

even thought for a moment about staying forever, at least until my pedicure chipped when I stubbed my toe on a rock.

So on my second—or was it third?—day in paradise, when the sun began to go down behind the hills, I pulled on some sweats and fired up the camp stove to cook myself a hotdog and some freeze dried mac 'n' cheese. To be honest, I wasn't even that hungry, but I wanted my experience to be authentic. And that meant cooking over an open fire. Even if it was just fueled by a little green can of propane gas.

After, I put away all my crap and hoisted my food into a tree, just like Pippa and I had learned, to keep the critters out of it. I crawled into my tent, where I added some more air to my mattress, and snuggled into my sleeping bag. I really didn't understand why anyone had a problem with camping. It was freaking awesome. In fact, maybe I could find a way to stay longer.

Nah, I had to get back to work at the shit hole.

Unable to sleep, too excited about my perfect day, I propped myself up on a little pile of clothes and worked on my song lyrics in the light of my mini-lantern, pleased as punch about what a great camper I was turning out to be.

I woke up to a soft patter-patter sound, and for a moment I had no freaking idea where I was. I reached around for a light in the pitch dark and when I fumbled for the switch on my lantern, nothing happened.

Goddammit. I'd fallen asleep with it on, and now the batteries had run down.

The good news was, I had extras somewhere in all my crap, but there was no way to find them in the pitch dark. Instead of freaking out, I laid back down on my mattress and stared into nothingness while the patter-patter turned into a driving rain, and the dome of my tent was buffeted by winds that were no doubt going to make a mess of the equipment I'd left outside the tent overnight.

Real Girl Scout I was turning out to be.

CHAPTER 2

JOELLE

I didn't get back to sleep for what felt like hours, not with the uninvited rain and wind doing a job on my idyllic little camping crib. I was equally pissed I'd let my lantern batteries run down. But hey, if that was the worst thing that happened…

I must have eventually dozed off though, because I bolted upright in my sleeping bag at a *thud* just outside my tent. I grabbed for the pepper spray I'd kept in my shorts pocket, and silently unzipped the front of my tent in time to see a wily raccoon doing his best to commandeer my food supply.

"Get the fuck out of here!" I shouted, waving my arms like a nutcase.

The raccoon took a leisurely look at me and waddled into the woods, in none too much of a hurry. I could have sworn he even rolled my eyes at me. Bastard.

But what I hadn't noticed was how my delightful home away from home had pretty much turned into a sea of mud. In my haste to jump out of the tent and go after the raccoon, my feet were now coated with in the gooey brown.

Goddamnit.

I did a three-hundred sixty degree circle to get a view of my campsite and found that most everything I'd left outside the tent, including the actual outside of the tent, was splattered in a mud-rain mixture of chunky little brown dirt dots, now hardening in the dappled morning sun. Worse off were the towels I'd hung on branches near my private swimming hole. Not only were they soggy through and through, but they too had drops of mud splashed up all over them.

I reached into my tent for my flip-flops, and padded down to the embankment where I doused my towels in the river, rinsing the worst of the mud before spreading them to dry over the rocks I'd sat on just the day before. I then dipped my feet into the stream and watched the mud slowly dissolve and float away. Ah, clean again.

That was, until I walked back into the campsite. But one thing at a time.

I bent to rub a little more dirt off my feet when I heard something like voices. I stayed dead still until I could confirm they actually *were* voices. My heart jumped into my throat and I took refuge behind a tree at the water's edge.

Who the hell had invited themselves to my private party?

They drew closer, and I watched from behind a tree where I was hidden with a perfect view of the hiking trail that passed right by my site. I wasn't sure exactly why I was staying out of view, but until I could assess my gatecrashers, it seemed the prudent thing to do.

I had my reasons for being on alert. It was a total self preservation practice, honed to perfection over the years.

Two male figures gradually came into view, and I could swear they were talking about something like the best way to preserve game or meat or game meat. I couldn't be sure. But damn if the two weren't a couple of the most hulking hotties I'd ever laid my eyes on.

Too bad I was compelled to hide. But a girl had to be careful about taking her chances. Especially for someone like me.

"Whoa. Check this out. Someone's camping here," a blond guy said, as they stopped to look over my stuff. "Damn shame about the mud. Gonna suck cleaning all that later on."

The other one, with delicious tattoo-covered biceps, nodded. "Wow. Didn't know people actually came up this far to camp."

They took a couple steps into my site and peered at my equipment. My hand was on my pepper spray in case any of the fuckers decided to help himself to my stuff. I was in the wilderness, and I was ready to fight.

Yeah, right.

"Looks like brand new equipment," one of them said.

You got that goddamn right.

"A little worse for the wear from last night's storm," the other noted.

They both stood, continuing to evaluate my stuff. *My* stuff.

Then they turned, looking into the woods, like they might find a clue about the owner of said camping equipment. I ducked behind the tree just as they turned my way.

The blond pulled his hands up to his mouth and began to holler, "Hallooooo. Is anybody there?"

Tattoo guy did the same. "Do you need help?" he called.

Silence.

"I guess we could wait here a bit. Or, look inside the tent to see if that tells us anything."

Without meaning too, the bastards were calling my bluff.

"Oh, hi there," I called, stepping from around the tree like I'd just appeared out of thin air.

Surprised, they both whipped around, their eyes wide.

"Oh. Hi," the blond said. "We were wondering whose stuff this was. Glad to see you're okay."

I stood on the edge of the campsite. *My* campsite.

"I'm good. Thank you," I said with my most polite you-can-leave-now smile.

"Okay. Awesome. We don't see many people camping around here. Actually, we don't see *any* people camping around here."

"Do you live in these woods or something?" I asked with a laugh.

They just looked at me.

Oops.

"This is public land. I have a permit I can show you," I said, moving toward my tent to prove my right to the property, if only for a few days.

"Hey, it's all good. You don't have to show us anything," the tattooed guy said, holding his hands up like a *stop* sign, and taking a few steps back, I guess to show he was no threat. "Just caught us by surprise, that's all."

"Guess last night's rain did a job on your stuff, huh?" the blond said, looking around and shaking his head. "Man, what a mess."

Thanks. Make me feel worse than I already did, why don't you.

"Yeah. My stuff is pretty much trashed. But I have a stream right here, so it'll be easy to clean up."

I wasn't about to let my guard down, but damn these guys were some tasty treats. You didn't see mountain men in Vegas. Or at least, not real ones. The best you could hope for was the occasional wannabe poseur, convincing enough until you caught a whiff of the aftershave in his perfectly combed out beard.

15

The blond was buff as hell, but also kind of preppy looking at the same time without looking too frat boy douchey. His T-shirt was off, revealing a six or twelve pack or whatever you call that, and was tucked into the pocket of his jeans, which, due to a lack of a belt, hung low on his hips. Damn if the guy wasn't going commando—I was pretty sure I could see the top of his happy trail, his jeans were hanging so low. His back-pack straps hung tightly on his shoulders and the chest strap pressed into his skin. His piercing blue eyes looked me over, and I wished I were a little more covered up than my shorts and tank allowed.

But how was I to know to expect company?

The tattooed guy, on the other hand, was not quite as tall, but his sleeveless T and hiking shorts displayed a collection of ink the likes of which I was sure I'd never before seen. He wore some fucking seriously high-quality tats covering both his arms and legs. His messy rock 'n' roll hair was partially pulled back into a cute little man bun, and the scruff on his face indicated he hadn't shaved—or even trimmed—his beard in awhile. The effect made my knees weak.

Especially since it was multiplied by two.

They seemed friendly enough, to be honest, so I decided to relax at least a little. "Um, I was just gonna heat up some water for coffee. Would you like to join me?" I asked.

They looked at each other like *why not.*

"Sure. Love to. I'm Pierce, by the way," the blond said.

"And I'm Jax," said the other.

"Nice to meet you," I said, stepping forward to shake hands. "I'm Jo. Short for Joelle."

They made themselves at home on one of the huge logs left behind by someone who'd arranged ample seating in the site, and I flicked on the camp stove and set the water to boiling. They conveniently pulled tin cups out of their backpacks and seemed satisfied with the freeze-dried coffee I made them.

"This is an awesome little place," Pierce said, looking around. "You've got a nice, flat clearing, and your own little watering hole over there... how long are you here for?"

I followed his gaze, nodding. "I know, right? I totally lucked out with this little spot. Anyway, I'm just camping for a few days. One of my girlfriends was supposed to join me but couldn't at the last minute, so I came alone."

Fuck. Why had I just announced to these two total strangers in the middle of bumfuck nowhere that I was all alone?

Good move, girl.

My hand wandered to the pepper spray in my pocket. Still there.

"Damn," Jax said, "you don't meet many women camping on their own." His head bobbed approvingly.

"So what are you guys doing up here?" I asked warily. It was their turn to do some telling.

Instead of immediately answering, they looked at each other.

What was that all about?

"Um, Pierce's family has a cabin. We're staying there," Jax said.

"Really? A cabin?" I'd not seen a cabin or any other kind of structure on the map when I'd gotten my permit. "Where's the cabin?"

Piece shrugged nonchalantly. "Oh, couple miles away. That direction," he said, gesturing with this chin.

Okayyyy…

I decided to let that one go. I had my secrets. They could have theirs. Whatever.

Maybe they were gay and just weren't 'out' with it. A darn waste of manhood in my opinion, but I couldn't fault them any.

I stood. "Can I get you more coffee?"

"That would be great," Jax said, holding out his cup. "Double strength?"

I got him a refill. "Sorry this is instant. I know it's kind of gross, but since it's my first camp outing, I didn't want to be too ambitious with a French press, and all."

"No problem. It's great," Jax reassured me. "Thank you."

"Here you go—" I said, hot coffee flying out of my hand as I slipped in the mud and landed flat on my ass.

What a way to make a first impression.

CHAPTER 3

PIERCE

In all the years that I'd been going up to my family cabin in the mountains, I'd never run into another camper. Well, except for Jax, but I'd invited him because he and I were buddies. But never had either of us just stumbled upon another person. The place was just too remote, my cabin a weird leftover title of private land surrounded by state forest that protected it from ever having neighbors. The location, while beautiful, really took some effort to get to.

This woman didn't just stumble across this place. She was there for a reason. A well-planned reason.

And Jo wasn't just *any* camper.

She was hot in the way that reached back and grabbed my balls by the memory strings as far back as my fumbling teenage years. With her daisy duke shorts and skimpy tank top, which, by the way, she was not wearing a bra underneath, she looked like the epitome of a country girl seductress. Her long, toned legs, bright eyes, plump bow shaped lips, and tight little nipples that stood out like a pair of diamonds against thin cotton just completed the image.

Shame to be wasting that on a solo camp out.

Christ, I sounded like a pathetic little horn dog teenager. But when you go weeks without seeing a woman, much less a *woman* like the one in front of Jax and me at that very moment, your heart beats a little harder, and yes, your dick stirs in a way you forgot it could.

And a woman camping alone? Now, that was ballsy, the likes of which I'd never seen. It made her even sexier, in my opinion.

And just as our new friend Jo was handing Jax another cup of her terrible instant coffee—seriously, I had no idea people still drank that freeze-dried swill— which we were suffering through only to extend our visit, she slipped in mud thanks to the stupid flip-flops she was wearing. Wiped the hell out and landed flat on her ass. She legit dumped hot coffee all over poor Jax who jumped up and started shaking the scorching liquid off his arms and legs.

What a mess.

To be honest, I almost laughed, it looked so slap-stick-y, but thank god I didn't. It took about five seconds to realize Jo was hurt and in pain, not to mention filthy from having fallen on the rain-soaked ground.

"Oh, shit, shit, shit," she yelled, trying to get some purchase on the slippery ground in order to pull herself back up.

I reached a hand to help, and it was only when she tried to maneuver to her feet that we noticed one of her ankles bent at a slightly strange angle. But the true extent of the injury didn't become clear until she tried to put weight on the foot. The pain must have been immense because her previously healthy color turned dead white, and she let out a screech that most likely frightened animals for miles around.

"Fuuuuuuuuuck!"

"Hey, easy there, take it easy," I said, grabbing her arm for support as she followed up with a string of expletives that would make a Marine Corps drill instructor blush. "Here, lean on me, keep your weight off of it."

Jax took her other arm to lower her to a seat on the log where he'd just been. "You know, you should really wear hiking boots at all times. They protect your ankles."

The look Jo gave Jax was deadly enough to kill a small animal at fifty feet. "Yeah, thanks. It's a little late for that now, though," she snapped.

I was sorry she was hurt, of course, but the fact that she could still manage to essentially tell Jax to shove his observation up his ass intrigued me even more.

"Goddammit," she yelled, picking up the closest rock and throwing it against the side of her tent hard enough that I'm surprised it didn't leave a tear in the nylon.

"I twisted my ankle and it hurts like a mother-fucker. Probably no ice for miles. Shit," she said, putting her hands to her face as if she could wish her way out of the predicament.

Her shoulders shook, and I knew she was trying not to cry, but twisting your ankle like that hurts… bad. No shame in crying, then, I wanted to tell her. But I didn't know her well enough to offer my opinion. Yet.

"I tell ya what," I said, kneeling down and putting a hand on her shoulders. "How about Jax and I help you down to the water? It's not ice, but it's cool and might help prevent some swelling."

I knew damn well her ankle was going to swell like a motherfucker, but hoped the water would provide a modicum of relief. It might have sucked as a first step in terms of treatment, but it was better than nothing.

"Y… yeah," Jo said, looking up and smiling wanly, tears still floating in the corners of her eyes. "Thanks."

She was light as a feather as we half-carried her to the water's edge and settled her on a smooth rock that allowed her foot to hang in the water. If it hadn't been for the very mud she'd slipped in, I could have handled her all by myself. The feel of her warm skin against my arms shot tendrils of sensation between my legs, bringing my dick to some serious attention.

When we got her settled, I stepped back reluctantly, and I think Jax did too. Jo sighed in relief before her face pinched.

"Okay. That feels nice," she said, mostly to herself before turning those doe eyes on us. "Would you guys mind getting me my backpack? I think I have some Advil or something."

"Um, sure. I'll get you some water, too." Jax and I headed back to her site.

When we were out of earshot, Jax spoke in a low voice. "Christ, what is she going to do now?" he asked. "She can't freaking walk."

I watched her swirl her leg in the water, like a little mermaid trying to decide whether or not to go in. Her blonde hair spilled around her shoulders, half pinned up in some sort of crazy sexy confection, and I had to control the urge to adjust myself in my jeans, which were feeling very tight at that moment.

"No shit." I asked in a low voice. The real question, however, was what the hell *we* were going to do. We couldn't very well leave her there.

Could we?

We could help her back to her car and load it up with all her crap, but how would she drive? She'd hurt her right ankle. You can drive a car with a hurt left leg, but right? No way.

And we sure as hell couldn't bring her back to our cabin... for a multitude of reasons.

"Dude, she's basically an invalid. We can't leave her here," Jax said. "She can't even walk the ten feet back to her tent."

I took a deep breath and looked at Jax.

I could tell he was thinking the same thing I was.

"If we bring her back to the cabin, Blaze will fucking lose his mind. There's just no way we could do that." I was half-hoping Jax agreed with me so I didn't have to be a fucker all by myself.

But Jax was never a fucker.

"Well, we'll deal with that when we have to. But for now, bringing her back is our only option. Aside from leaving her, which I could not do," he said.

Shit. Why had I gone out for a hike with the nice guy of our group? He was forever bringing back hurt animals. Now, a hurt human.

Jo gulped her Advil with a big water chaser, and winced when she pulled her foot out of the water long enough to see it had already begun to swell to an angry shade of pink-purple.

"Guess I'll be cutting this trip early," she said, looking around sadly. "Fuck."

"How are you going to do that?" Jax asked, rubbing his chin, and taking the opportunity to peek down her loose top.

She shrugged. "How do you think? I'll pack up my shit and go home. I was so stupid to think I could camp like some kind of goddamn expert. What did I think I was doing?" She pressed her temples with her thumb and forefinger.

Jax crouched in front of her. "Jo, you can't stay here alone."

"I'll be fine. Thank you for your concern, but I can manage," she said dismissively.

Well, if she wanted to be such a bitch about it, we'd leave her… problem solved.

But not so fast. "Okay," Jax said, standing up and using a tone of voice I'd grown so familiar with. His 'I'm right, and you're being an idiot' tone.

"Show us. Show us how you'll be fine on your own. Show us how you'll get out of that water right now and how you'll make your way to your tent. Show us how you'll manage to make something to eat."

He held his hands up, waiting.

Not happy about having been called out, Jo started to stand on her good foot. But the minute she put weight on the bad foot, she nearly fell to her knees in pain.

"I… I can do this. Just give me a sec."

She put her bad foot down gingerly, and slowly transferred weight to it.

Bad idea.

"Fuck that hurts!" she exclaimed, following it up with a litany of other scream-level swear words.

"Yeah. Sprained ankles are no joke. And that's what you have." I put my arm out so she could lean on me. Christ, she smelled good—and she probably hadn't had a shower in a couple days. I'm not a sniffer, but she smelled honest, sexy, and just… womanly.

"Well, fuck me. I mean, what the hell am I going to do now? I should have just stayed home. Not gone anywhere, and not tried to prove that I was a badass who could camp alone in her own brand-new tent, her own brand-new sleeping bag, wearing her own brand-new hiking boots. God, what a loser."

Well, that proved my first impression correct. And she was right, she never should have gone camping alone. Never mind the mud, there were plenty of other challenges and dangers in the mountains that weren't for tenderfoot soloists. But if she hadn't given it a shot... we'd never have met her.

"Jo, I think what you need to do is let us bring you to our cabin until you're well enough to get home," Jax said. "It's not far."

Unlike Jax, I was worried about what the other guys would say. We had pretty clear rules about life in the cabin, and they didn't include hosting guests. But what the hell were we supposed to do? Leave her there to rot?

It would be a hard sell, convincing the other guys to put up a stranger for a few days. But when they saw how hot she was... that should help. God willing.

Or it could turn into a scene from National Geographic with a bunch of alpha males beating their chests and fighting over the attention of the female in their midst. That was an option too. Especially with who all was at the cabin.

Jo shook her head. "I can't do that. I mean, what about all my stuff here?"

Jax and I looked at each other. "We'll take it with us. Pack it up, and take it with."

She really didn't have that much stuff. Besides, if she'd packed it in, we could pretty easily pack it out.

"What do you say? We can set you up on that log right there, and you can tell us how you want it packed up. Then, I'll wear your pack, and Pierce will be your crutch."

Defeated didn't begin to describe the tragic expression on her face. Humiliation maybe. Possibly utter shame.

"How far is it to your place? Will it take long to get there?" she asked, probably imagining ten miles of being thrown over my shoulder like a sack of potatoes.

Not my style, though. I'd carry her like a gentleman. To be honest, if I had to carry her for days, it wouldn't be enough time to spend with her.

Shit. I had it bad.

CHAPTER 4

JOELLE

Well, fuck all.

One little slip, and that was the end of my camping excursion.

And now, I'd just gotten an invitation to whatever sort of creepy bachelor pad my new buddies called home. Their *cabin* I think they called it. I could only imagine.

Pepper spray in front pocket. *Check.*

Last will and testament filed? I knew I'd forgotten something.

But my ankle hurt like a sonofabitch, and evidenced by the way it had already blown up, and my inability to put even a scant amount of weight on it, I was lucky the guys had happened by.

'Course if they hadn't, I might not be trying to

impress them with my camping coffee skills and have fallen on my ass to begin with.

But seriously. What would I have done if I'd hurt myself and was all alone? My cell phone sure as hell didn't work there.

Too scary to think about.

"You sit there on that log, and we'll pack up your stuff for you," Jax repeated, as if the decision was made and I'd given them my orders. Christ, he was a sweetheart. I could tell he was probably the 'sensitive one' of the two. Speaking of which...

"How many people you got in your house—I mean, cabin—anyway?" I asked.

"Four. There are four of us," Pierce said as he disassembled my cooking gear and organized it in a way I didn't know was possible. Seriously, he broke it down and fit it together in a nested little bundle that made it even smaller than what I'd found in the package in the store.

"All dudes?" I asked. Might as well know what I was in for.

"Yup," he said, not looking up from his work.

Christ, this would be the end of me. They were probably serial murderers, and in twenty years they'd find my bones in some backwoods canyon or ditch, my friends like Pippa relieved for the closure and that they no longer had to worry I was 'out there'.

Pepper spray wasn't going to do a damn thing against four of them. Not even the bear strength variety.

Basically, I was fucked.

But for some reason, I couldn't say no. I didn't *want* to say no, like if I was gonna go out, I might as well do it as dramatically as possible with all this eye candy around me.

I was pretty sure quite a few girls in horror movies died with the same thoughts in their empty ass heads, and I just couldn't help myself to a bit of my own drama.

"Jo, I'll pack up your tent now," Jax said, wisps of hair flying out of his adorable man bun, a sheen of sweat glistening on his tattoos. He crouched to look inside, noting how I had my crap spread out all over the place in a royal mess. Cripes.

He'd have to put all that back together for me. I certainly couldn't do it.

"Okay, first let's get the sleeping bag and mattress," he said, gently pulling them out without letting them touch the muddy ground.

For a serial murderer, he sure was tidy and nice.

Maybe I was just freaking out a bit too much about dying in the woods.

And in a flash of his skilled hands, he had the two items compressed into their little travel bags and attached to my frame backpack.

"Okay," he said, wiping his hands in satisfaction. "You have a lot of other stuff in your tent. Don't mind me saying, you might have over packed."

It was true.

"You can just throw it in my backpack, if you don't mind."

"Pierce, let me hand you the stuff in her tent and you can put it in her pack. Here," he said, passing him a T-shirt, my sweats, and a couple pair of dirty underwear.

Oops.

"Oh, hey Pierce. Don't forget this," Jax said, holding my vibrator between his forefinger and thumb.

Fuck.

They both turned to me, unsuccessfully suppressing smiles as Jax lifted an eyebrow.

Whatever.

I shrugged. "You can throw that in the bag, too." What difference did it make?

Yeah, I enjoyed a good orgasm as much as any woman. That I'd been using a little mechanical advantage instead of a good old-fashioned dick said more about the quality of men I'd been meeting than anything else. I didn't have time for embarrassment, and in the meantime, I was getting a kick out of directing these two hot-as-fuck dudes, who were sweating and flexing as they took my tent down.

If only I could have taken some pictures for Pippa. And really, all the girls at Maid to Order. They'd never believe the direction my big adventure had taken.

Which got me thinking about how all my hard work up to that point in life seemed to have been for absolutely nothing, if these guys were indeed going to do me in. There'd been no demo tape. All the songs I'd written sat on my hard drive in my apartment, lyrics written in Word files and tunes plunked out in Garageband. A lot of effort sitting around doing nothing, sort of like I was right then.

In the meantime, I was going to enjoy the view and file it away for a song if I lived long enough. The way the shirtless Pierce's jeans hung low on his hips, showing off that heavenly 'V' only a few, select men seemed able to pull off, was giving me plenty of inspiration.

He stood, hands on hips, and looked around my site. "Well. Looks like no one was ever here."

All the better to cover up my impending murder.

Jax nodded. "That's what I call a good camper. Leave no trace behind. We wish everyone were as considerate of nature as you, Jo."

I smiled, setting my foot down and reminding myself that nature, at least in the form of water falling from the sky, could quite happily go fuck itself.

Pierce helped me hobble to standing as Jax effortlessly hoisted my pack onto his shoulders like it weighed nothing. Shit, I'd had to struggle with the damn forty-pounder.

Guess it was time to turn in the yoga mat for that Crossfit membership Pippa kept bugging me about.

"Okay Jo, so lean on me, and I'll put my arm under yours on your bad side. That way you can use your good foot without putting weight on the bad foot."

His strong arm scooped under my arms and around my back. His skin was warm and slightly damp from the labor of breaking down my campsite, and I'll be damned if he didn't smell great. Not like hair gel like the guys who came to Maid, but a clean sort of great. Fresh, healthy, with the very slightest scent of man sweat.

"Okay, step like this," he said, demonstrating how he was going to half-carry me through the woods. His gaze wandered up to mine but he stopped midway when we both realized my braless nipples were poking against the thin cloth of my white T-shirt.

Nothing I could do about it now. And I liked the tingle anyway, it matched the growing one between my legs.

And when he saw me catch him looking, I could swear a tinge of pink passed over his face, and his gazed snapped back down to my feet to make sure I was moving my one good foot in rhythm with his two.

Clump. Clump. Clump.

About as ungraceful as a person could get. It was like doing a three legged race with a giraffe, as big as he was.

But hey, I was being held up by the hottest freaking outdoorsman a girl could imagine—tall, strong, shirt-less, and actually almost pantless too, with the way his jeans were hanging.

He glanced over his shoulder. "Jax? You back there with Jo's stuff?"

"Right behind ya, bud."

And so it went for what seemed like an eternity, but was really probably only an hour, on a path that was overgrown to the point of being almost unrecognizable unless you knew it was there.

Pierce and Jax certainly knew it was there. But if I had to retrace my steps, or somehow find my way out of these mountains without their help, I'd end up a bear's dinner in no time.

Didn't matter. I was more relaxed with Pierce at every step, and while I wasn't sure I could trust them yet, I at least felt good enough that I wasn't going to end up as a side character in some Lifetime channel movie. And despite the pain of my hobbling and the slow, exhausting progress, at least I was with two hunks of the lumberjack variety.

Shit, they could probably take on a pissed off momma bear, and walk away with a new fur pelt to tell their story.

Yeah, they were all *that*.

"You need a rest, Jo?" Pierce asked after a bit. Guess he'd seen the perspiration running down my temple. I prayed he hadn't felt the sweat coming off my under-arms, too.

"How much further is it?"

"Not far," he said, directing me to a log. "But I need to take a leak."

He stepped into the woods, declaration and decision complete. My ass was sitting for a few minutes.

I looked up at Jax from my perch. "Thanks for carrying my stuff."

He shifted my pack as if to assess its weight, and shrugged, giving me a pretty dazzling smile. "It's no problem. I'm used to carrying much more than this. But Pierce was right, you do have a lot of stuff for just a few days."

Geez. Rub it in a little bit, why don't you? I got it, I'm not the kind to walk in with a canteen, a Swiss army knife, and a pair of tube socks expecting to walk out just fine three days later. I liked my little comforts, and maybe I'd overdone it a little.

"Was that really a hair-dryer in the bottom of your pack?" he asked.

"Well, yeah, I mean I was thinking that in case I decided not to camp and instead to go a hotel—"

Oh why was I explaining?

We stared at my ankle, now a swollen, angry reddish-purple.

"Ready guys?" Pierce asked, returning from the woods. The sunlight behind a cloud cast a shadow, somehow making him look all the sexier. Every muscle on his chiseled torso sprang out in full relief, and I could nearly trace the curve of his veins under his biceps.

Actually, I would really, really have liked to.

Christ, I couldn't believe such a hunk had just had his arm around me. And was going to again.

If these guys were going to cart me off into the

woods, maybe I'd just stumbled onto the greatest camping adventure of all time.

I'd do a little happy dance if I had two feet to do it on.

Pierce pulled me to my feet—or should I say *foot?*—and I got back to hobbling.

CHAPTER 5

JAX

Pierce might have appointed me pack mule by suggesting I carry the lovely Jo's camping crap, and he carry *her*, but I was the one who lucked out.

Walking behind the two, I had the pleasure of watching the cheeks of her ass under her tight—and very short—khaki shorts. It was like she ordered a camping outfit from Victoria's Secret or maybe central casting, designed by someone who thought they knew what someone might wear in nature, but had never been there, herself.

The end result was anything but practical. Her cheeks practically hung out of her shorts, flexing and showing off her muscles as she jump-hopped. But she wasn't overly fit, giving me just enough jiggle to imagine her flesh quivering as she rode my hard dick. The vision left me raging hard in my pants.

Not that I was complaining. Believe me.

And when she'd sat down for a little break, I'd had to adjust my boner in the face of the hard nipples swinging under her lightweight shirt, and the way her shorts outlined her pussy lips.

Down boy.

Yeah, it was pretty evident I'd gone too long without a woman.

And to make matters worse, Jo was exactly the kind of woman you'd want to find stranded in the woods, in need of help from two nice guys like Pierce and me. Her camp-messy hair and smooth, lightly tanned skin were driving me wild, even if she hadn't been dressed in that 'naughty camper' costume.

What the hell would she have done with a twisted ankle if Pierce and I hadn't happened by? On the other hand, if she hadn't been making us that awful coffee crap, she might not have slipped to begin with. So, in a sense, I guess it was our fault she had gotten injured.

Not that we wouldn't have helped her anyway.

And now that I was looking at a beautiful woman in the flesh—curvy ass and nice little tits—I realized that my regular jerking off to the same old porn mag was losing its luster.

Ha, maybe she'd want to repay me for carrying her shit by getting down and dirty. In my mind, I could see myself peeling those too-tight shorts over her ass to expose a bare pussy dripping with excitement—

Jesus, I needed to get a grip on myself. Thank god I

was walking behind her and Pierce because there was no hiding my hard wood now.

And her backpack—who took all that shit camping? She'd brought her vibrator, not that I could blame her —a little fresh air turned me on, too. But, because I was lucky enough to have packed her shit, I'd seen her damn hair dryer.

Really?

I was going to give Pierce some serious crap first chance I got. The bastard had cockblocked me after all, looking down her shirt every chance he got. Lucky for him, he was wearing blue jeans so his own hard on— yup, he had one—was kept somewhat under control.

Christ, if the girl knew how long it had been that either of us had had a woman, she'd go running in the opposite direction. If she'd been physically able to.

What if she hadn't hurt herself? I suppose Pierce and I would have hit the road after a few more cups of lousy coffee, and headed home. Probably done a lot of bragging, and a little surreptitious monkey spanking. But I can promise one thing—I would have found my way back there to pay a little visit the next day.

Maybe she would have been up for a little swim or hike, or would have let me teach her about wilderness survival.

But why bother fantasizing about that crap? Fact was, I was now carrying all her shit on my back, and we were heading home.

Which might not have been the best idea in the world.

"Halloooo," Pierce called when we hit the clearing where our house sat. "We're back."

The front door swung upon, and Reid stood before us. "Yo, guys, I thought you might be the—"

Not surprisingly, he stopped short when he saw an extra person with us. A very lovely extra person.

We climbed the steps to the front porch, where Reid stood, speechless, looking from one of us to the other.

"Hi, I'm Jo. Nice to meet you." She extended her hand like she was in a freaking business meeting or something.

Reid just stood there, staring at her. He seriously looked like his brains had just shut down, and he was ready to throw the circuit breakers, fall to the deck, and go into reboot.

But Jo was undeterred and threw her head back, laughing and assuming, like pretty girls always did, that she was welcome everywhere she went. "I guess you don't see many strangers around here. Especially women."

It took her a moment to realize Reid might not have been too happy to see her. And that's when things began to get awkward.

"Reid, Jo hurt herself at her campsite, so we brought her back here," Pierce said, pointing at Jo's swollen ankle. He pushed past Reid and into the house, settling the issue before Reid could be a dick about it.

"I have all her stuff here," I said, gesturing to the pack I was wearing. I needed to say something.

"Uh, yeah. I can see that, Jax," Reid said slowly. He

still looked like he was in overload mode, and I wondered, when he was fully back on board, if his reaction would be good, bad, or catastrophic. Before he could respond though, Jo once again seized everyone's attention with her magnetism.

"What a cool house." She took in the place with a three-sixty-degree turn, holding on to Pierce the whole time, while Reid looked like he was trying to quell an explosion of temper.

"Let me show you to my room so you can get your foot elevated," Pierce said, throwing Reid a dirty look, and disappearing down the hall with the hobbling Jo.

"This is her stuff here," I said, shaking off the pack. It was sort of a repeat, but I didn't know what else to say.

"No shit," Reid said. "I know you didn't leave the house with that on your back." Peering down the hall, he saw them turn into Pierce's room. Reid knelt and began unzipping the pockets on the pack, and before I could say anything, was diving into the main compartment.

"Dude, would you relax a little? I packed this thing, so I know what's in it," I said.

Reid stopped and looked at me. "There wasn't anything strange? Nothing suspicious?"

"No man. Unless you consider a battery-powered vibrator something to be concerned about."

"Well, what the fuck, man?" he growled in a loud voice.

Loud enough for Jo to hear down the hall, and it

was my turn to give Reid a good 'STFU' look.

"We are not a halfway house for damsels in distress," he hissed.

I raised my hands like a *stop* sign. "Dude, seriously? She can hear your big mouth. So maybe you can quiet down a bit."

He shook his head violently. "Hell no. We don't do house guests here."

I pulled him outside, onto the front porch, and got in his face. Sometimes you had to do that with Reid. "Look, she twisted her ankle when we were in her site, talking to her."

"What the hell were you doing in her campsite? Why didn't you just head in the other direction before she saw you?" he asked.

"Don't worry about it. And stop being such a dick. There was nowhere else for her to go, and we were just trying to be friendly. So deal with it. Besides, it will do us some good to have a female around here for a few days."

Reid's eyes widened. "Oh, I get it. You took her in because she's a hot piece of ass. Okay, now it's all clear."

Nodding like he knew everything, he slammed his hand onto one of the front porch posts, shaking dust and cobwebs from the ceiling onto our heads.

"Oh get over yourself, Reid. You know… you can be a real asshole sometimes." I swung the door open and went back inside, where we found Pierce.

He hiked up his too-low jeans, pulled his T-shirt back over his head, and put his hands on his hips with satisfaction. It was beyond me why the dude never wore a belt.

"Okay, she's on my bed with her ankle propped up. I got her some ice, too."

Reid's head snapped in Pierce's direction. "You what? We don't have ice to spare. You know that."

Pierce and I looked at each other and rolled our eyes. Ice? Fucking ice was his problem?

"Reid, would you calm down—"

"Um, excuse me gentlemen." Jo's voice came from the living room doorway, where she held the wall.

We'd been so preoccupied with Reid's acting like a little bitch that we hadn't heard her making her way down the hall.

There she stood, now wearing one of Pierce's fleeces, still clad in the short shorts that showed off her shapely legs. She looked directly at Reid, and I could see in an instant… she was pissed.

"In case you are living in a fantasy land, what makes you think I *want* to be here any more than you want me to be here? I don't know you people, and despite Pierce and Jax being nice, I don't trust you guys. And now I want to be here even less, as if that were possible."

She looked from one of us to the other as we stared, speechless.

And I loved watching her give Reid a taste of his own bitter medicine. I hoped he'd choke on it. Asshole.

But she wasn't done. "Forget you guys. I'm leaving." She turned back to her room, hopping on her good foot and using the wall for support.

Yeah, she wasn't going anywhere. It'd take her half an hour just to get out the front door.

I followed her back to Pierce's room, trying to make some peace. "Jo, I'm sorry about Reid. He's a hothead. I recommend you just ignore him because, look at yourself. You might want to get out of here, but that's not gonna happen. You need to be lying down, icing your ankle."

She spun around and pointed a finger in my chest. Damn, she was feisty. And fuck, was that sexy.

"You have a car, don't you Jax? I mean, how the hell do you guys get here?"

"Well, yeah, we have trucks, but they're not close by. Just like your car was not close by. We gotta hike out to them."

Her shoulders sank and she closed her eyes as she shook her head. "Great, just great. I'm really and truly fucked."

She hung her head like a wilted flower, and I realized she'd begun to cry again. This time it wasn't physical pain, but a simple case of a young woman scared, offended, angry, and more. It just overwhelmed her, understandably so.

"C'mon, Jo. Let me help you back to bed so you can relax a little."

She nodded without raising her head and lifted her arm so I could support her. We clomp-clomped the rest of the way down the hall, with her sniffling, and me trying to hide my huge hard-on.

CHAPTER 6

JOELLE

What a bag of dicks those guys were. Well, not Pierce or Jax, they seemed nice enough, but I hadn't received a warm welcome to the cabin at all. If my ankle wasn't fucked up, I'd be out of their shitty little house so fast their heads would spin.

And that Reid. The nerve of his comments. Like I *wanted* to impose on them. Pierce and Jax had practically begged me to go there with them. And Pierce half carried me up the hill, anyway.

Uh, hello, you tools. I'm here because I had no choice. You, my new asshole friends, are pretty much my last choice right now.

'Course they were also my *only* choice. Because despite my repeated comments to the opposite, there was no way I was walking out of there and back to my car. I'd be lucky if I could make it to the potty without having an accident.

Fuck. How long would I be stuck there? I'd never had a sprained ankle. Maybe I could head out in a couple days? God willing.

The thoughts were still running around in my head when Jax came into the bedroom, giving me a hopeful smile. "How's the swelling?"

"I think it's getting a bit worse," I admit, looking down at my leg. Yup, no way was I winning the sexiest legs competition at work with that purplish blob going on. "What can we do?"

"First we'll elevate it, and if that doesn't work we'll wrap it," Jax said, peeling back the thick fur blanket on the sprawling bed that was Pierce's. He grabbed a huge pillow and bunched it under my bad ankle.

His words were so kind, and he seemed so sincere, I couldn't help but smile a little at him. "Thank you Jax. I'm really sorry to be imposing on you guys. I'll be out of here as soon as I can."

The front door slammed so hard the house shook. Jax rolled his eyes and laughed.

"That was Reid. Don't worry about him, he finds something to have a shit fit about at least once a week. And as for your staying here, just relax."

"Where will Pierce sleep?" I asked.

Jax turned around in the doorway, scratching at his chin with one finger before answering. "He'll either bunk up with me, or sleep on the sofa. Depends on

48

how bad he's snoring." He chuckled and closed the door behind himself.

What a freaking day it had been. I looked around Pierce's room, decorated in a kind of lumberjack, cabin-in-the-mountains chic with exposed beams, heavy paneling, dramatic paintings, and dusty books lining the shelves on the walls. Depending on how long I was to be there, I might borrow a book or two to pass the time. I was nearly done with my dog-eared copy of *Fifty Shades of Grey*, which had been circulating among the waitresses at Maid.

Pippa was next in line for it and wasn't going to be happy when she realized her turn would be delayed by my accident.

Drowsy, I reached under the covers and peeled off my filthy shorts and top, and as I dropped them to the floor, I saw an old wooden box peeking out from under the bed.

Curiosity might have killed the cat, but I wasn't a cat. And I had pepper spray, anyway.

I cocked my ear toward the door, and from what I could tell, I was alone in the house. Guess the guys were out felling trees and trapping bears, or whatever it was that mountain men did. I tried lifting the box up to the bed, but it was too heavy to manage, so I slowly lifted the lid.

Have you ever been surprised, yet not surprised, at the same time?

The contents of the box were along those lines—

and consisted of different sized dildos and a greasy bottle of lube.

Well. Who would have thought Pierce was such a dirty little dog? But who also would have thought a tall, blond, wholesome-looking dude would live in the freaking mountains and run around shirtless with his pants practically falling off?

Obviously, I didn't know shit.

I tipped the box to see *all* its contents. God knew I didn't want to touch any of it. But I did see paper underneath his pervy sex toys, and when I pulled on it, found it was a porno mag.

That specialized in *anal*.

Yowsa. Serious dirty boy.

And something about that got me hotter than hell. I let the lid close and my hand wandered to my pussy, which was by now fairly throbbing. My fingers wandered through the silky wetness in my folds, settling on my clit, where after rubbing a couple little circles on it, I exploded in an orgasm that left me convulsing and banging my head against the pillow behind it.

And it didn't hurt that I'd pictured Pierce sliding his jeans down his slim hips to expose a rock hard dick, and Jax between my legs licking away. I'd even let the jerk Reid in on my imaginary deed, where he rubbed his cock on my tits before Pierce took over for a deep fucking.

I might have had a messed up ankle, but I was warm, dry, and safe—at least for the time being. Not having slept well the night before thanks to the noise of the storm, I drifted off and dreamt about fucking each of my new mountain friends like a horny bitch.

I couldn't get enough, and of course, neither could they.

My sex dreams came to an end all too soon, and I woke up to sun streaming into my room—well, Pierce's room—and muffled voices from other parts of the house. I hadn't seen much of the place the day before when I'd arrived other than the living room and the hallway to Pierce's room, but I was pretty sure the source of the conversation was another bedroom, or maybe an office.

Do mountain men have offices?

I guess I'd pretty much dropped the serial murder paranoia, fun as it was to imagine my days would end surrounded by gods like Pierce, Jax, and Reid. But now my mind was racing with *why* the hell these guys were living in the middle of bumfuck nowhere. I could see a temporary visit to the wilderness to get back to nature and all that shit, but it looked like these guys were seriously entrenched in the house.

Like, they weren't going *anywhere*.

Who does that?

People on the run, that's who. I could relate.

I peeled back the fur throw on the bed to get a look at my injury.

Um, yeah. Based on the colors decorating my poor ankle, I wasn't leaving today. And probably not tomorrow, either.

Shit.

My previously slim lower leg was now a dark splotchy purple, swollen beyond recognition all the way down to my chipped pedicure toes. I reached for the water and aspirin Jax had placed on the nightstand, and gulped three tablets as fast as I could.

Hobbling with just my good foot, I managed to get out of bed to pull some clean clothes out of my pack, which Jax had also thoughtfully placed at the foot of the bed on top of a wooden chest. Just as I was digging out some new undies, the bedroom door flew open, scaring the shit out of me.

I shrieked.

It was Reid.

Now, if I were to walk in on someone getting dressed or doing something else that normal people consider private, I'd excuse myself, apologize, and take my leave.

Not Reid.

He walked into the room as if I'd invited him, looking my bare-assed self up and down, pausing when he saw my natural thigh gap and pussy, which still felt puffy and engorged from my hot dreams.

I pulled a T-shirt out of my pack and attempted to hide my lady bits while balancing on one leg. "Yes, Reid?"

He cleared his throat, and ran his fingers through his long beard before holding up a stick, or a board, or something. It looked like an uppercase T with a knob attached about halfway down.

"Morning, Jo. Wanted to bring you this crutch. The guys and I put it together for you. It's not perfect, but… well, it should help, right?"

Was he really speaking to me as if I were fully clothed?

"Um, I was getting dressed," I said, gesturing toward my pack.

Realization passed over his face, and for the first time he looked normal, not so haughty or pissed off. "Right. We aren't really modest around here."

Okay then… if I looked like they did, I guess I wouldn't be modest either.

If he wanted to act all cool about nudity, I could play that game. I dropped the T-shirt that wasn't really hiding much anyway, and just stood right there in front of him, butt-naked.

Undeterred, he continued. "I want to apologize for being… difficult yesterday. I'm glad we can help you. We're just not used to strangers here, and I guess… it threw me off."

Well, it was an apology. Didn't quite make up for the rest of his issues, but it was a start.

"Um, okay. Can I go back to getting dressed now?"

CHAPTER 7

REID

I placed the crutch we'd made for Jo where she could reach it, should she decide to use it.

"Yeah, please, get yourself dressed there. Guess I should have knocked." I averted my gaze and started backing toward the door after feasting my eyes on her fucking hot little body. I was a sucker for a tight ass and small tits, and this girl had that in spades.

Damn her, she looked like my favorite teenage crush.

Now all I was going to be able to think about was getting in her pants. If she managed to put any on.

"Your ankle looks bad. I can get you some more ice, if you like," I called, unable to stop sneaking glances. And she knew it.

She was finally dressing, but slowly. Like she was putting on a show. The little vixen, if I didn't know better, I'd swear she was teasing me. Maybe she was getting her fifty cents of revenge for the way I'd acted the day before.

Either way, I felt a stirring in my pants that I hadn't felt in a long, long time. Too long, really.

"You were very rude yesterday," she admonished me lightly, lifting an eyebrow.

Okay. A woman who called me on my shit. Another secret bit of Kryptonite to me, one I'd kept everyone in the world from knowing.

"I was rude, you're right. I'm sorry."

If I could re-do the day, I would. But it was too late for that. I *could* make changes going forward, though. I mean, we all made mistakes, right? And some of us made more than others.

Like me.

That's how I ended up in the woods, to begin with. Making mistakes.

The family business had been good to me. Until it wasn't.

My grandfather on my mother's side had built a small hotel empire in New York City, with our first property on Times Square. There were lots of ups and downs over the years, but my father and uncle took over the business when Grandpa died, and I went to work for them right out of college.

Those were heady years where I was paid a lot and

ran around the city like a party boy on fire. I fucked models, actresses, and princesses, and partied with all the city's young masters of the universe. Not everyone in my crew were household names, but enough of them were that my posse was the envy of the East Coast.

It wasn't all bright lights, big city.

I worked my ass off, constantly innovating to keep the hotels' competitive edge. You see, the more models, actresses, and princesses we had staying at the hotels, the more everyone else would come running. It was a lot of work to keep that edge, but we did it.

One Thursday I was at our downtown property making sure all the details for a birthday party for one of Mick Jagger's daughters was in order. People like that spent a lot of money with us, and brought us even more business. There was no room for error—any of the hundreds of other top tier New York hotels would eagerly jump in to take our place at any moment— when I got a call from my dad.

He didn't sound good.

"Reid, I can only talk for a couple minutes," he'd said.

"What's up, Dad?"

"I'm going down to the police station to turn myself in."

I'd been sure he was just joking.

"Dad? What the hell are you talking about?"

"There is a warrant for my arrest. The attorney just called me about it. If I turn myself in, that will look better than waiting for them to come to me."

I laughed. "Dad, is this supposed to be some sort of bad joke?"

One of our very sexy secretaries dropped off my lunch—a rare filet mignon and a Caesar salad—and walked away, shaking her ass and looking over her shoulder at me in a way that usually made my dick twitch. I hadn't fucked her in a while.

Maybe she'd be free later...?

But it wasn't going to happen, not that day.

"No, Reid." Dad's voice cracked. "I've made a mistake. A terrible mistake. The attorneys will tell you all about it, but in a nutshell, I misused some of the company's cash. The cash that came from investors."

"You did what, Dad?"

"I have to go. I'm sorry, Reid. I'm so sorry." The phone line went dead, but almost before I could check the news, my cell started ringing.

"You fucker, Reid, you and your father stole our goddamn money," growled Demian, one of our business partners and son of my father's best friend.

Former best friend.

And that was the beginning of the end. Dad had not only been pumping up the bottom line to keep stock prices high, but had shifted money around, lying to investors. He was hauled in front of the courts, and it made plenty of headline news as he pled guilty and got five years in Federal prison.

The unrelenting shame and guilt, not to mention losing a business that had been in our family for generations, was too much to bear. The moment I'd ceded my family's interest to the bankruptcy court, I'd gotten the hell out of dodge.

No reason to stick around.

Jo's expression softened at my apology, trusting I was sincere, and I was smart enough to look away while she finished dressing.

"Thanks Reid. Thank you for the crutch and thank you for apologizing."

She lowered herself to the edge of the bed, sighing from the exhaustion of dressing and standing on one foot at the same time. She hadn't invited me, but I went back into the room and sat next to her.

"I have to admit something, Jo."

She cocked her head. "What's that?" She lay back on the bed and propped her foot back up on the pillow.

Ugh. Time to convey what an absolute dick I could be.

"I think one of the reasons I was pissed when I saw you was that you were so beautiful, and I thought the other guys would have you for themselves."

Her mouth fell open for a moment, and then she dropped her head back with a laugh. Then she shook it, her hair flying all around her lightly freckled face.

"Yeah. That's what I'm here for. I really came just to fuck all of you. The sprained ankle? Just an act to get inside your mountain cabin." She laughed again and I felt like the idiot that I was.

"I know, I know... teenage thinking. I'm sorry about that."

"Well, I have something to admit, too," she said.

She looked down, almost like she was shy. But I wasn't fooled. The girl was tough as nails, although I knew that sometimes it took courage to share what was really on your mind. Or in your heart.

"I... I... fantasized about all you guys last night. I haven't been able to stop thinking about how long it's been since I've been with a guy, much less freaking gorgeous, strong men like all of you. I mean, I don't know any of you from Adam, but I can see you've built lives for yourselves up here, and that can't have been easy. Takes some guts. And sacrifice."

Well. I'll be damned.

Taking a risk, something I hadn't done in a long time, I ran a hand up her thigh, her thick sweatpants between my palm and her warm skin. Maybe if I played my cards right...

She didn't stop me. Instead, a sly smile spread across her face, and she pressed up into my hand as if she were offering consent.

But before I could move closer to the sweet juncture of her thighs she stopped. Backed off.

"Um. Don't think this is a good idea, Reid. You know, now that I think of it." She placed her hand on top of mine to halt my stroking.

Well, any idiot could see her hard nipples poking through her pullover, and notice the scent of her sex. Her turned-on sex.

I took her hand in mine, stroking it from wrist to palm to fingertips, and then turning it over and doing the same to the soft skin on the back. I didn't look at her, but instead just focused on that hand. When I did look up, I saw she'd leaned her head back on her pile of pillows, and closed her eyes.

I let my fingers wander up her inner arm, pushing her sleeve as I went, and when I couldn't bunch the fabric anymore, my fingers moved to her neck, which I stroked completely—front, back, with my fingers and thumb, soothing, massaging, and eventually, gently squeezing. I watched as her breath picked up and her lips parted slightly.

I took the opportunity to run my rough thumb over her lower lip. When she parted her lips more, I pulled on that sweet, red lip, and pushed my thumb into her mouth, which she puckered her lips around and began a slight draw.

Well, shit. That was all I needed. I dropped my hands to the waistband of her sweats, and shimmied them down her curvy hips. I parted her legs lightly and buried my face in the mound between her legs, inhaling her scent through her lace panties, kissing the insides of her thighs.

I looked up at her for a sec and she smiled, putting her hands on my head to direct my attention where she needed it most.

I nosed aside the lace that covered her privates, and got my first up close look at the most delicious, shaved pussy I think had ever been crafted and placed upon a female form. Her lips were swollen from her excitement, her little clit hard as a rock. I ran my tongue from one end of her to another, lapping at her ass, her juicy hole, and back.

Her hips bucked in time to my strokes and when she was soaking wet, I entered her with two of my fingers, letting her adjust while I relished her tight, clingy walls.

Now, I knew my hands were rough and my fingers thick, so I held them deep inside for a minute. Then, I started to pull my fingertips forward in a 'come here' signal, finding that button that I knew was there. That was about all the girl needed, because her body contorted into a strong arch, her head thrown back, pushing her hips so hard into my hand that she nearly broke my wrist, all while I made gentle strokes on her clit with my tongue.

"Oh… oh… fuck… I'm coming. I'm coming," she cried in a breathy yell, her hands running over her delicious little tits, pulling and squeezing the nipples.

I pistoned my hand in and out of her juicy hole, eager to draw things out for her. I knew she'd be sore later, but I didn't care. I wanted to give her the orgasm of her lifetime, and I wanted her to remember me the next day every time she went to sit down. I wanted her so raw, she had to sit in a bath of ice cubes, her pussy was so beat up.

I wanted her to never, ever forget me.

CHAPTER 8

JOELLE

Jesus Christ. I'd never had anyone send me into mindless bliss like Reid just had. I was still convulsing when he took his lips off my clit, and moved his fingers to my mouth where I could lick them clean. The taste was so nice, salty but also soft and sexy, just like I felt at that moment in time.

And for a few minutes, I wasn't even thinking about my aching ankle.

He drew himself up next to me on the bed to hold me as I caught my breath, very careful of my ankle.

A noise came from the front of the house, and Reid bolted upright.

"What is it?" I asked.

He cocked his head as the front door opened and then slammed shut. "Wait here. And don't make a sound."

He hustled to the door, which he opened a small crack. Not sure what he saw out there, but he inched out, pulling the door soundlessly closed behind him.

I yanked my underwear and sweats back up and straightened my shirt.

Some loud voices were now yelling. I couldn't make out what they were saying when Reid ran back into the room, again closing the door behind.

"Hey, you need to get up," he whispered. "Get all your stuff."

Was he kidding? I was operating on one leg.

"C'mon," he said, half carrying-half dragging me toward a closet.

Great. I get to hide in a closet? Maybe the guys *were* serial murders, and I'd just been given my last orgasm. How nice of them.

Reid yanked open the closed closet door, pushed aside a bunch of hanging clothes that smelled of cedar, and reached for the handle of another door in the back of the darkness. The new room we entered was pitch black but it seemed he knew his way around—he settled me into some sort of easy chair, and propped another chair under my foot.

Then he dashed back in with my backpack.

What was all this? A panic room? A place to stash your... stash? What the hell was I getting into?

"Here's a flashlight," he said, thrusting one into my hands. "But don't turn it on."

And with that, he was gone. He pulled the hidden

door closed and I heard him moving the hanging clothing back in place. Then, the outer closet door closed, followed by the bedroom door.

I wasn't a fan of sitting in the dark, but I didn't know what harm would come of turning on the flashlight. So I dug into my backpack and found my cell phone, which would provide illumination, but only a small amount if I were careful.

I flashed my phone around from where I was sitting, and while the light didn't shine very far, I could see I was in a comfortable little room with a twin bed, a desk, the easy chair Reid had put me in, and a shelf full of books.

These guys really loved their books. I couldn't quite make out the titles on the spines, but they certainly didn't look like light reading. At least, I didn't think anyone made a leather bound copy of *Log Cabin Living For Dummies*.

I heard more loud voices, and clicked my phone off. I didn't want to risk anything. I leaned back in the chair, unable to make out the conversation.

They were probably talking about what a slut I was for messing around with Reid, and putting together a schedule so they could all have their chance with me.

Then, they'd murder me.

Actually, I was no longer worried about that part. The murder part.

And what did I care if they thought I was a slut? I was on vacation for Christ's sake. I'd never see these guys again, once I got out. No, rugged mountain guys were not a regular part of my life. I mean, I was happy to stay at their house, eat their food, and mess around with one or two of them, but when I got back to Vegas, I'd forget about them in five minutes.

And that was fine by me. Every girl deserves that one weekend where we got to live out a couple fantasies, and then highly edit them for later story telling.

And I could barely wait until I told the girls at Maid about them. They'd be green with envy, how I had my own little man harem for a couple days.

Yeah, I'd be out of this place in a couple days. Right?

Bored, I grabbed for my phone again, even though I wasn't supposed to use any light. I was thinking of every way I might get a message to Pippa, but there was no network available for wifi, and my cellular service, not surprisingly, didn't pick up any signal. This place was a hundred percent off the grid.

Shit. I couldn't call, text, or send an email.

I was well and truly fucked, as they say.

Just then the closet door flew open. I hadn't even heard anyone coming. I clicked my phone off, but it was too late. Someone shone a flashlight right in my face, and growled like an animal.

"What the fuck are you doing? You were told not to turn any light on."

I don't think so. "Um, sorry. Who are you? What's going on, and why am I in a hidden closet? Why don't you answer those questions before you raise your voice to me?"

Yeah, I could be a bitch when I needed to. Considering some of the clients I'd had to deal with, I'd had excellent training at Maid.

I pushed myself up from my chair using the crutch Reid had given me, and when I got closer, I could see the jerk screaming in my face was a new guy altogether —not Pierce, Jax, or Reid, not that any of them would yell at me like that, anyway.

He was taller than the three guys I'd already met, completely bald, and had some sort of tattoo on the side of his neck. It was a little hard to see in the dim light, but he had one of the meanest faces I'd ever seen.

Which pissed me off even more. I had no use for bullies.

So I pulled myself up to my full height, leaning on the crutch, and got in his face.

But it didn't do any good. The dude just doubled down.

He took a breath, and spoke slowly and clearly. "You were told not to turn any lights on. I don't know what was so hard to understand about that, but you did it anyway. You put all our lives in danger." He turned to go but I caught his arm.

He whipped back around to face me, shocked I had the nerve to touch him. But I didn't care. There was no reason I should be treated that way. I'd done nothing wrong. Well, except for letting Pierce and Jax bring me into their little freakshow of a life. Talk about a mistake to regret.

Now I was *really* getting myself worked up.

I poked my finger into the guy's chest, which was rock hard with muscle. He could have broken me with one swat, but I didn't care.

"I didn't want to come to your home, or whatever the hell this place is. In fact, if you could see it in your heart to find me a lift somewhere, I'll gladly be out of your hair. *FOREVER!*"

Fucking dick.

By some miracle of time, space, and just being pissed off, that shut the creep up. Yup, his mouth actually dropped open, and he didn't have a goddamn thing to say.

Before I could ask him the main question on my mind, namely who the hell he was, Reid, Pierce, and Jax appeared behind him.

I was on a roll, so my rant kept going. Great orgasms or not, eye candy or not... I was not taking it.

"Oh, great. There's the rest of ya. Are you going to let me out of this closet? Or are you keeping me prisoner? Huh?" I screamed, pushing the new guy aside, and addressing the ones I'd already met.

And in Reid's case, had basically slept with. He at least had the wherewithal to look a little chagrined.

Pierce raised his hands like a *stop* sign. "Okay, Jo, you need to take it down a notch. Listen, there's a lot going on here, and obviously this hasn't been the best way to bring you into the scene."

"No shit."

"Let's start over, then," he said in a placating voice. "We'll fill you in as much as we can. C'mon. Let's talk."

He reached to assist me but I jerked away from his hand, preferring to hobble with my crutch.

I was done with their help.

CHAPTER 9

BLAZE

After my initial shock at being scolded by the mouthy chick who couldn't follow a few simple instructions, I grabbed her by the shoulder and spun her to look at me. Too late, I realized my mistake as she nearly fell.

The other guys all reached to keep her upright, since she only had one good foot, but I was quicker, and set her straight.

"We need to know, Jo, that next time we make a request of you, like to get in the closet, remain silent, and in the dark until we tell you it's safe to come out, that you can comply with our wishes. If you can't do that, we're going to have to ask you to leave right away. Figure out on your own how to get down the mountain and to your car."

As if she doubted my ultimatum, she turned to the

71

other three guys, the ones she'd met before me. If she were expecting them to side with her, she was on the wrong track. They all looked at her and shook their heads, agreeing with me. Even Reid, who'd just been eating her pussy—I could tell by the musky scent he was carrying.

And the way he'd been smiling.

Instead they all looked at her, reinforcing my message. I knew they would. We had a carefully built mini community that functioned perfectly. We didn't take for granted that a big part of part of what made it work was agreeing to a few basic rules.

Like no visitors.

So much for that.

But maybe I shouldn't have been so hard on her. It's not like she knew what a quiet life in the mountains meant to each of us.

We were all there for different reasons, and we knew that. We'd reached a certain level of peace with our different paths, and we were secure with each other.

The important thing for her to understand was that there was nothing that was going to get in the way of our continued peaceful existence. Nothing, not even a hot piece of ass. With a big mouth.

On the other hand, I could relate to being mouthy in the face of authority, just like Jo. It was a survival mechanism—one that worked at times, and backfired at others.

My own big mouth had led to my living right there on Savage Mountain, if I went back far enough.

I'd been an insolent kid. Got in tons of low-level trouble. Nothing too horrible, but my dad had no tolerance for any amount of nonsense, and sent me off to Green Valley Military Preparatory Academy when I was fifteen. He was determined to *set me straight* as he liked to say.

Little did he know that instead of being paragons of discipline and feeders for upper crust universities, military schools were full of juvenile delinquents.

And when you got a bunch of barely tamed delinquents together, they fed on each other. Festered really, like rapidly growing mold.

Any innocence I had when I entered military school disappeared almost overnight, when I was beaten down after lights out by my very own 'team leaders'. I quickly learned that Green Valley was like being in a prison with its own underground economy and unwritten rules.

And I learned how to be just as predatory as those around me.

I wasn't a bad kid when I went in, but I sure was when I got out.

Thanks, Dad.

Lucky for me, one of my teachers had taken a liking to me. Somewhere he saw some potential in between my smart mouth, shoplifting episodes, brawling, and cheating on tests. God knows I didn't deserve any special consideration, but he connected me with a 'group' he was acquainted with from his own past, before he'd decided to educate punks hiding behind tidy uniforms and polished shoes.

I was offered a job starting at a hundred grand a year, no shit. I'd never made more than five dollars an hour, when I'd worked at the school cafeteria, and I had only a freaking high school degree.

They didn't care. So I didn't care.

At first they told me I was going to work for an NGO, or a non-governmental organization. I had no idea what that was, nor did I care. I just wanted the damn money. And what sounded like riches beyond my wildest dreams quickly became something I had to work hard for.

Very, very hard.

I learned I wasn't really working for an NGO, which was a fancy name for an international charity, like Doctors Without Borders, or some such. There was no charity involved in what I was doing, and very little organization.

No, I'd gone to work for a private military contractor, or in simpler terms, I'd become a mercenary. Turned out military schools like mine, full of juvenile delinquents with few to no other options, were the perfect recruiting ground for 'private security' teams, as they were called. Led by men who'd gotten actual military training and found civilian life too 'pussy' for their tastes, the methods employed were harsh, brutal, and straight to the point.

And there began my career as a PMC. I never really knew who the client was who hired me to do this or that in some far-flung location, but I learned the rules, and did my job well.

Rule one, you protect your team's back at all times. Even before the client, you cover your team's ass.

Rule two, you fight hard, and party harder. The shit we got up to in some of the far off places was stuff of legend. I don't know if we caused more damage with a gun in our hands or without.

Rule three... don't ask why the fuck you're getting paid. Just be happy you are, and kill whoever you're told to kill. And that I could do, quite well in fact.

I did things I wasn't proud of, but I saved my money, figuring that after a few years of work I could disappear, and hopefully be set for life.

Things had almost worked out that way.

After one particularly hairy deployment to Central America, I decided that I'd had enough of the merc trade, which made my employer none too happy. In fact, the only way most guys usually left the business was either in a wheelchair with a severe disability, or in a coffin.

No one exactly 'retires'. So when I turned in my paperwork, there were certain things said. Nothing that would stand up in a court of law of course, but I knew the lingo. I knew that if I wasn't careful, my truck was liable to explode. Or my water heater. Or just damn, ain't it a shame how young men are killed every day by guns in the U.S.A.

So that's why I'd taken my ass up to Savage Mountain and kept a low profile at Pierce's place. He'd also been in the PMC world, and was also done with being a merchant of death.

Up there though, we could keep our heads down, and keep a low profile. A very low profile. And I protected my new life like it was all I had in the world, just like the other guys in the cabin.

It pretty much *was* all I had.

When I'd grabbed her arm, Jo turned toward me with a look of terror on her face. I felt a little badly about scaring the shit out of her, but a hardheaded girl like her needed to know we were serious as a heart attack. Especially a pretty girl like her. They always thought they were above the rules, spoiled as they were by society, just for their looks.

Yeah, I knew her type. I'd been with plenty of pretty babes like her, not being a bad-looking guy myself, and other than a fun fling when I was willing to pay, I'd been kicked to the curb by almost every one. The last thing this girl was going to do was fuck me up. Her stupid pride could go to hell.

She seemed subdued, finally, or at least scared shitless. At the moment, I didn't really care which.

"Listen, I don't understand what's going on. I'm

sorry, I had no idea it was this serious." She looked around nervously.

"I don't know what you guys are up to, and I'm not sure I want to know, but I have no intention of creating any difficulties for you. I apologize."

Tears shone in her eyes, and she rubbed them off with the back of her hand. When I stepped back, she returned to the bed and propped her foot back up on the pillow. She took a deep breath, lay her head back, and closed her eyes.

"Guys, let's give Jo some time to rest," Jax said, ushering all of us out of the room. "Jo, can I bring you some toast for breakfast? We have some fresh-made bread."

Her eyes popped open. "Seriously? Fresh baked bread?"

Jax smiled, nodding. "We make our own."

Jo's lips twitched in a grin. "You may have found my kryptonite. I'm still pissed, but fresh baked bread... might help."

The guys and I filtered out to the kitchen, an extension of our large living room, and I started cutting the bread I'd baked that morning. There was an eagerness to our movements that I hadn't seen in a long time... and I wondered if the cause was what I suspected.

Reid shook his head, and spoke in a low voice. "Blaze, not sure you had to come down so hard on her. I mean, she's a nice girl."

Pierce piped in. "Not to mention fucking beautiful. Man, the ass on her—"

I put my hands up to silence the praise of our uninvited houseguest. "You guys are some of the thirstiest motherfuckers on the planet, you know that? Look, I know we don't see many women like her—or many women at all, for that matter—but stop thinking with your little heads. You sound like a bunch of idiots. We are not a way station for inexperienced campers. We have a lot at stake here."

Pierce rolled his eyes, a move that *really* pissed me off, and he knew it. "Blaze, for fuck's sake, get off your high horse. You sound like a freaking lunatic."

Jax and Reid started to laugh. "Yeah, man. Chill out."

Fury rose through me, but I was determined to control it. "If you guys don't get rid of her in a few days, I'll do something about it. And it won't be pretty."

I hated to be such a dick, but some things were just not negotiable.

Not when our safety... shit, our fucking lives could be at stake.

CHAPTER 10

JOELLE

In spite of the earlier blow up, the guys were being nice about checking in on me, laid up as I was in Pierce's bed. Poor guy, I'd put him right out of his own room. He didn't even complain about it, just said he'd grab a few items when he needed them, and the couch was fine for now. Talk about a sweetheart.

Almost all of them were, to some degree.

All the guys except for that hateful, brutish Blaze. God, he was a psycho, getting in my face and threatening me. I'd backed down out of self-preservation. But when I had the chance, when I was back on my own two feet, literally and figuratively, I'd give him a piece of my mind. Maybe even kick him in the balls.

And I'd thought Reid was a bit of a jerk, at least initially. He was Mr. Nice Guy compared to Blaze.

After several hours of icing my disgusting-looking

79

ankle, I was beyond stir crazy. I'd finished *Fifty Shades*, finding it mildly titillating, and had plowed through half of *The Great Gatsby*, which I'd already read several times but could never stay away from for very long.

I wouldn't have minded playing around with writing some song lyrics, but my strange situation had zapped the creativity right out of me. Hopefully it would return ASAP.

In the meantime, something delicious-smelling was cooking, and I was dying to get out of the room I'd been cooped up in. The toasted bread from the morning had been to die for but now I was hungry again.

But I had to say, the thought of joining the rest of the guys in the living room, as if I were one of the gang, was kind of intimidating. Normally, I was pretty comfortable in every situation, but the circumstances under which I was at that house were unusual, and it had been made clear I wasn't exactly welcome.

Which was really kind of shitty, if you asked me.

But cripes, did Blaze really think I was just going to hole up in that room the entire time I was there? If so, he had another thought coming.

Still, I hesitated. I just did not get the drama behind why I'd been stuffed in that secret closet, and how I'd risked all their lives by using the light on my cell phone. It'd be really nice for one of them to fill me in and explain what the hell was going on—but on the other hand, maybe it was just better that I not know.

Jax had made it seem like he'd talk, maybe explain

their strange set up and secret closet, but Blaze had shut that down quickly. I wasn't sure about pushing that button again.

What if they were like, weed growers who were just trying to keep their crop secret or something? Or mafia guys on the run? I wasn't there to rat anybody out. They could do what they wanted without my interference.

Still, a little background might keep me from screwing up again. It's always better to know the rules up front, right?

I got up and hobbled out of the room, and I saw Blaze over in the kitchen, stirring a giant pot over what looked like a wood stove. I decided I'd work on him first. Make friends. Flirt a little.

"That smells great, Blaze."

He looked over his shoulder, startled by my voice, and grunted. He ground some fresh pepper into the pot.

Okayyy...

I was not easily discouraged. "What is it? That you're cooking?"

He didn't look my way, but at least answered my question. "Fresh venison. Jax took down a deer yesterday."

"Oh, that sounds great," I said enthusiastically, repressing the urge to gag.

I have never understood the appeal of shooting cute little Bambis. But that's me.

I looked from the kitchen and Blaze, to the guys in

the living room. Christ if they weren't a hot bunch, all of them. Powerful and masculine, so much so that it made my knees week. They were each striking in their own way—Pierce with his blond surfer-boy look, Jax with his wild black hair and rock 'n' roll tattoos, Reid with his tidy beard and man bun, and even dick-head Blaze with his shaved head and imposing size.

And yet, they were clearly a team that worked together toward a shared goal. They really had built a little nirvana on top of Savage Mountain. It was pretty amazing, if not a little strange.

What sort of person runs away from the world? One with something to hide, that's who. Which meant I probably should not have been mixing with them. But they were so goddamn manly. Any one of them could have broken me in two, which terrified me and turned me on at the same time.

And those damn naughty dreams I'd had...

"Anything I can do to help? Got any dishes to wash? Potatoes to peel? I'd like to earn my keep," I said earnestly.

And foolishly.

Blaze snorted and mumbled something like *oh you will* so softly I couldn't be sure that was what he said. But it was hostile and passive aggressive, and I bit my tongue to keep from telling him off. I wasn't exactly in the best position to pick a fight, even if it was with the world's biggest and most deserving asshole.

"Yo, Reid, could you go get some more firewood?" Blaze called over his shoulder.

Reid set down his book. "Sure. Be right back." The door slammed behind him.

Pierce also set down his reading material. Guess they did a lot of reading around there. Made sense, considering they didn't have a television, and the only electricity I'd seen was a small solar panel that probably could barely charge a single LED lamp.

"How long 'till dinner?" he asked.

Blaze stirred the pot again and poked at the ingredients with a long wooden spoon. "It's gonna be awhile. I want to make sure the meat's nice and tender. I'd say at least an hour and a half, still."

"Okay. I'm gonna go bathe then," Pierce said.

Jax tore his gaze off me and said, "I'm going to clean up, too."

Without looking, Blaze waived his hand in the air, as if giving permission.

That left me alone with someone who clearly was still not interested in talking to me.

"If you'll excuse me, I'm going to go use the bathroom," I said.

"We don't have a bathroom," Blaze growled.

Technically, he was right. They had an outhouse. But did I have to call it that?

"Be right back," I said.

The cool evening air felt good after the tension Blaze had stirred. Not only was he not willing to have a conversation with me, he seemed to be the cause of the silence of the other guys.

I followed a short path to the outhouse, lurching

along without an ounce of grace thanks to balancing between one good foot and a makeshift crutch that took some weight off my bad ankle, but not all of it.

After I'd taken care of business, I realized I heard Pierce and Jax's voices coming from the other side of the house. As rustic as the place was, it was also pretty big, and in my weakened condition, I'd not really checked the grounds out. Nor did I dare.

A simple thing like turning my phone on had nearly caused my eviction. Couldn't take any more chances like that.

But my curiosity had gotten me in trouble before. Looked like it just might again.

Lucky for me, the ground was covered in a soft bed of pine needles, so my approach was mostly silent. When I finally had a clear view around the corner, I saw a giant hot tub and a big steel drum on its side. On one end, the drum's open door revealed a small wood fire, and on the other, a pipe extended from it, into an opening on the side of the tub.

That must have been how they heated the water.

So now I understood how they bathed—in a giant tub warmed by a wood fire. Good lord, they had it all figured out.

Pierce and Jax were soaping themselves up— couldn't say I'd ever thought I'd see two guys bathing together, but I could have watched them rub their bodies with soap for hours. In fact, I wouldn't have minded helping them, not at all. I moved closer as stealthily as my lame condition would let me, and damn if I didn't step on the loudest branch in the forest.

Snap.

The guys' heads turned in my direction, but because the woods were somewhat dark, they couldn't see me. Thank goodness.

"Another raccoon," Jax said. "Too bad they make such awful eating. We'd have enough food to last forever. Little bastards."

Ew. They'd tried raccoon?

"I know, right? Those little shits are so easy to catch and they're freaking everywhere."

Jax leaned back in the tub to rinse his hair one more time. "Okay. I think I've had enough. Gotta leave some clean water for the other guys."

Sharing bath water was what you did in the mountains, I gathered. But hey, what if I wanted a bath? I was dying to yell out *don't forget about me*, but I didn't want to reveal my spying.

And boy, was I glad I kept my big mouth shut. Watching Jax get out of the water, dripping wet with steam rising off his skin, was almost worth the pain and inconvenience of a sprained ankle and a ruined camping trip.

Of course, I'd checked him out earlier when he was helping me to the cabin. But as he stood before the fire to dry off, I got a glimpse of a very hard and shapely ass, and when he turned in my direction, I saw a nice long cock that swung against his muscled thigh.

He reached down to dry his balls with his towel,

and then pulled his jeans back on, making his way to the house.

Holy fucking hell. When I'd calmed my thudding heart I realized I was gripping the tree I was leaning against so hard my fingernails hurt.

That shit had been worth the price of admission. I made a note to find a way to get my hands on that ass before I hightailed it out of mountain town.

And now it was time for the Pierce show.

He splashed water over his shoulders and he, too, stepped over the wall of the tub while cupping his balls, I guess so he didn't smash them on the tub's edge. He then bent with his ass facing me and lowered his head close to the fire to shake out his hair, leaving nothing to the imagination.

After a minute of running his fingers through his hair, he rotated before the fire much as Jax had, giving me a show of his hard, lean physique.

He wrapped a towel around his waist, and headed for the house.

Well, now.

I leaned back against the tree to catch my breath, and looked up at the stars. With absolutely no light pollution, there were nearly more twinkling lights up there than actual sky. It was brilliant, literally and figuratively.

For a moment I forgot I was stranded on Savage Mountain and that my camping trip had been thwarted all because I was a klutz.

I heard a noise and turned back to the tub. Pierce had returned to stoke the wood fire.

This was my chance.

I lurched out of the woods as casually as I could, which isn't saying much.

"Oh hi, Pierce. Whatcha doing there?" I clump-clumped over to him.

"Hey. This is where we get ourselves clean, in this wood-fired tub. I have to add more wood to keep it warm for Blaze and Reid." He looked at me, puzzled.

"Were you just wandering in the woods by yourself?"

"Oh, just getting some fresh air," I said breezily.

"Actually, gotta admit, I was sort of wandering around after using the outhouse. It's very... rustic up here, isn't it?"

Pierce chuckled. "Well, be careful in the dark."

His shoulder muscles moved deliciously as he added more wood to the fire, and when his little bath towel opened a bit, my heart pounded.

I dipped my fingers into the water. Perfect. Just like the man in front of me.

"May I take a bath, too?"

He stood from stoking the fire, the wet bath towel draping nicely over his... well, everything.

"Yeah, of course. Sorry I didn't think to offer. If I were you, I'd get in now, before Reid and Blaze. They're both really into the whole outdoor exercise thing. After they bathe, the water's always disgusting.

Want me to help you get in? You know, because of your ankle?"

I couldn't wait to submerge myself in the warm water. "You're probably right. I will need help."

"Okay," he said.

We stood there looking at each other for a moment.

"Um, so are you getting in?" he asked, tilting his head toward the tub, looking me up and down.

Oh. Duh. Clothes.

"Um, yeah."

I propped my crutch against the side of the tub, and kicked off the one hiking boot I was wearing. Pierce politely looked away, pretending to stoke the fire, while I removed my sweatpants and top.

The cool night air slammed my bare skin, turning me into a solid mass of goosebumps, and all I could think was to get in the water as fast as possible.

But I couldn't. I needed help.

"Uh, I'm ready," I said, whipping my panties down to the ground.

He turned back toward me, his eyes automatically looking me up and down. Instinctively, I put a hand in front of my crotch, and slouched a bit as if that would hide my boobs.

"Can you look away, please?" I asked.

He quickly turned, but I could swear I could see him blush even in the moonlight. "Yeah, sorry 'bout that. Here, take my hand while you climb over."

"Thanks."

I hoisted my bum up on the edge of the tub, and

with my weight off my feet, swung my legs over. A quick look at Pierce confirmed he wasn't checking me out, at least not as blatantly as he had been. Then I slipped.

Because, of course.

"Whoa, hey there. Careful," he said, whipping back around to grab me with both hands.

He caught me before I fell off the edge of the tub and lowered me into the water as if I weighed nothing.

"Well, that was fun." I sank into the water where he couldn't see me.

Was there no privacy in the damn place?

CHAPTER 11

PIERCE

I can't blame Jo for not knowing mountain etiquette, but when she didn't holler for me to help her back out of the tub after fifteen minutes, I knew it was time to clue her in. I slung a towel around my neck and headed back to her.

"Hey, Jo," I called from a distance so as not to surprise her.

She leaned her head back on the edge of the tub, pointing at the stars. "Oh hey. This is heavenly. I could stay here all night."

No shit. That was exactly the problem.

"Well, we try to keep our baths to five minutes or so. It uses a lot of firewood to heat the fire. And unfortunately, that wood comes the hard way."

She bolted upright, her little tits bouncing in the water. I tried not to stare, but damn…

"Oh my gosh. Why didn't you tell me? Shit. Now Blaze will hate me more than he already does."

She stood and extended her hand for my assistance, in her panic apparently having forgotten her nakedness.

I helped her down from the edge of the tub, and there she stood before me, dripping wet and naked as the day she was born. She'd piled her long blonde hair on top of her head in some sort of tangled knot, and the tendrils that had escaped were wet and clinging to her neck and shoulders like seaweed on a mermaid.

It wasn't until she began to shiver that I realized I'd been staring.

"Here, sorry, I brought you a towel." I draped it around her back and began to vigorously rub her shoulders to warm her up.

"Thank you," she said quietly, looking down. Her last vestiges of modesty seem to have flown out the window.

"Hey, before we go in, can I ask you a question?"

I knew this was coming. It was inevitable.

"Sure."

With one hand on the tub for balance, she reached for her clothes and held them before herself in a bundle. The towel I'd pulled around her fell open, so I grabbed its sides and pulled it closed for her.

She looked so small and vulnerable at that moment —wet, clumsy, and no matter how tough she tried to act, completely out of her element. I wanted to take her in my arms and—

Down boy.

She looked up at me with the question on her face. God, I wanted to pull her towards me and taste those pretty red lips.

"It's best that you not know," I said. Yes, leave it at that.

But one look at her and I realized *she* wasn't going to leave it at that.

"Look. I'm staying here. I deserve to know if my life is in danger. If anybody's life is in danger. Because Blaze sure acted like we all were."

I shook my head. "No—"

A coyote in the not far distance howled and Jo lurched right into my arms. I say lurched, because that's all you can really do when you have only one leg to stand on and are trying to keep your towel closed while holding a bundle of clothing.

"Hey, calm down. It's just a coyote calling out to his pack. They don't bother with humans. We're way too big for them to mess with. You gotta get further north, to the actual wolves, to worry about that sound."

She pulled back as quickly as she'd jumped on me.

"Right. I knew that. I actually love coyotes. They're so cute. First time I ever saw one, in fact, I thought it was just a mangy looking dog… "

Her nervous babbling was interrupted by Blaze.

"Hey, is she ever getting out of that tub? Some of us would like a bath too," he hollered, going back into the house and slamming the door behind himself.

"C'mon. Let's move to the porch so the other guys can do their thing."

Fumbling with her clothes, she was pretty much hopeless. In the end I helped her hobble just like I had when I'd brought her to the cabin.

Was it a mistake to bring her here? At first, I'd thought it made perfect sense. I mean, who could leave such a hot girl in the wilderness when she couldn't walk?

But on the other hand, I hadn't anticipated how much strife the decision would make. Perhaps Blaze was right that having her at the cabin had put us all in danger—more danger than we usually were in, that was. I'd known the man a long time, going back to his and my early mercenary days when we were still pretty much kids, and I didn't think I'd ever seen him as rattled as he'd been earlier.

"Okay," I said, helping Jo up the porch steps, and over to where an old swing hung from the ceiling. It was dim in that corner, and I hoped it would help her relax and listen to what I needed to say.

But first things first. "Let's get you dressed before you catch your death."

I took her top and held it above her head to get her covered. She dropped the towel, and raised her arms obediently, which was even hotter in its own way. She looked so goddamn hot with a big, baggy sweatshirt falling off her shoulders, barely long enough to cover her privates, petite and adorable and sexy and... perfect.

The urge to take her flooded me again, this time my dick waking up and reminding me to get moving.

So I went for it.

With both of us on the old swing, I put my hands on either side of her face. "You know how fucking beautiful you are?"

In the dim light I could see embarrassment wash over her face, but it was quickly replaced by something I liked to think was a reciprocal attraction, and maybe even permission to *show* her how I felt.

Only one way to find out.

Slowly, very slowly, I pulled her to me just until I could feel her breath on my lips without touching them. She smelled like fresh, clean girl, sweet and minty, and I wanted her, dammit.

All restraint went out the window as I pulled her to me for a lush kiss. She responded eagerly, placing her hands on my head to pull me closer. That was all I needed.

My hand wandered down to her naked thigh and under the sweatshirt until I found a breast. It was small but ultimately, femininely sexy, with the perfect teardrop shape—heavier underneath, and with slightly upturned nipples. I pinched and pulled her little points, taking turns moving between the two, and she arched into me for more.

Fuck, why had I waited to do this? She'd been sleeping in my bed for Christ's sake. Alone. And I'd been jerking off on the sofa.

I slipped my hand down her back until I could grab

a handful of her ass, pulling her toward me to get her off the chair. Her booty was curvy and fleshy and I wanted to bury my face in it when we were somewhere other than the front porch. God willing.

The front door opened and closed and Reid and Blaze made their way to the tub, not even noticing us at the end of the dark porch. That made it all the hotter. I was fucking going for it.

I released Jo's ass and began to finger her pussy, which by now was hot and dripping with excitement. I ran my fingers in and out of her folds, and brought a finger to my mouth.

So. Fucking. Good.

No surprise there. She was as sweet as she looked, and I could feast on her candy for hours.

I parted her legs to improve my access, when she asked, "Hey, what if the guys see us?" She looked around nervously.

"What if they do? I don't care." I brought my hand back to her pussy where I notched two fingers at her opening. She shifted her hips forward very slightly, and I entered her, initially slowly, and then violently, because we both needed it—we needed release, we needed connection, we needed some fucking *fucking*.

I pistoned her little hole with my fingers, and she dropped her head back and held on to the chair as if it were going to take off.

"God, yes, Pierce, fuck me like that with your hand. Fuck me hard," she said in a hoarse whisper.

"You like it, baby? You like my hand in your pussy?

Are you a bad little mountain girl? Fucking yourself in your tent with that dildo?"

"Yeah…" she breathed. "Fucking needed it."

"I thought about you last night when I stroked my dick. I imagined lubing up your hot ass and sliding back and forth between your cheeks—"

"Oh… oh… fuck. I'm coming." Her legs moved as far open as they could get and she bucked her hips against the thrusts of my fingers as I gave her something she'd never forget.

I held her as she came down, her head falling heavily into my chest, my dick straining hard against the fly of my blue jeans. But I'd take care of that later.

"We need to get your foot elevated. Let's get you dressed and back in the house. You can get something to eat and then go to sleep.

"M'kay," she said dreamily, letting me help her step into her panties and sweats.

I guided her inside and was pleased to find she'd pretty successfully mastered use of the crutch we'd made her.

We sat down at the dining table, where Jax had pushed his plate away and had his sketchbook open.

I went to the kitchen to get us both bowls of Blaze's delicious cooking. Say what you will about that pain in the ass guy—he could cook some seriously amazing shit. The man was a certifiable backwoods gourmet.

"Whatcha working on, Jax?" I asked him, glancing at his work as I took a seat next to him and across from Jo.

"Huh? Oh, nothing," He slammed his book closed, and smiled. "Have a good soak?" he asked mischievously. "A nice, quiet cleansing?"

Okay, so he'd probably heard us on the porch. But I could seriously give a fuck, that's how much I cared. And Jo looked... not as embarrassed as I'd thought she might be.

"Mmmm. What is this?" she said with a weak smile.

I had a feeling she wasn't going to like game meat, but I couldn't be sure. "Stew a la Blaze. Never the same pot twice."

She giggled, and stirred her bowl. "I think Blaze said it's venison? I've never had it before."

"Blaze works magic with his limited supply of ingredients," I said, winking at Jo. "You've never had better."

She blushed, and turned back to her dinner, but it wasn't two seconds before her toe sneaked up my pant leg.

Yeah. My kind of girl.

CHAPTER 12

JOELLE

Oh. My. God.

Pierce was hotter than I'd even imagined. Those lips, and the way he touched me. That *tongue*. Cripes, I couldn't stop smiling. I'd have to find a way to get him alone again. I needed more of what he was serving.

Same with Reid, but one at a time, okay?

I couldn't believe what had happened. I wasn't that kind of girl... but at the same time, I had no regrets. I couldn't rank one of them above the other, I just knew I wanted both of them again. And again. And again.

I was starving, and they were just what I was hungry for.

Speaking of which, Blaze had prepared some sort of meat concoction, which the guys really seemed to like.

99

It did smell good, if you're into that sort of thing. Which I was not.

"Hey, um, do you think I could have some salad or something green?"

Jax looked up from his book, and Pierce's fork stopped mid-air.

Oh shit. Did I say the wrong thing again?

"I mean, the meat looks *great*, don't get me wrong, but I prefer veggies." I smiled politely, and looked from one guy to the other. I reached for a little piece of bread, although I normally tried to limit my carbs, but who didn't have a weakness for fresh bread?

I remembered a couple pieces of fruit in my backpack. I'd munch on them later. Salad first.

"Um, Jo, we don't have salad."

Huh? No salad? How the hell did they keep from getting scurvy or some other horrible disease related to lack of vitamins?

"Oh. Okay," I said with forced cheer.

Jax, ever the sweetheart, smiled kindly. "We really don't, Jo. Sorry. We usually have fresh stuff for the first week after we make our trek into town, but because it just doesn't keep, we only buy so much. We do have some canned beans, a few preserved fruits. Stuff like that."

Huh. Nothing fresh.

Pierce winked at me. "Sorry, Jo."

Well shit. I took a bite of the venison. And then another.

My mother had always said to take three bites of something before you decided you didn't like it.

But I didn't need a third bite.

Game meat in saucy gravy wasn't my thing.

"No worries," I said cheerfully, poking Pierce in the leg with the toe of my good foot. "I need to get my leg elevated anyway." I winked at him, wondering if he'd join me later. Or maybe Reid. Or maybe the two?

Christ, they must think I'm a huge slut. The cabin was small enough I was sure they all knew exactly what I'd been up to.

"Hey, one more thing, where's the best place to dry my hair?" I asked.

Once again, the guys stopped what they were doing and just looked at me.

"What? Did I say the wrong thing?" Again?

Jax responded with his patient smile. "We have limited electricity from our panels, and the generator's just for backup, and only for the most basic of things. Hair dryers wouldn't be on the must-have list."

Oops, I'd done it again. I threw my head back and laughed hard to cover my embarrassment. "Oh gosh, that makes perfect sense. I don't need to dry my hair anyway." I twisted the loose hairs back up into my bun as nonchalantly as I could, determined to keep quiet before I stuck my foot in my mouth again.

"No worries, Jo. You haven't done this before, this remote living thing. There is a lot to learn," he added.

I looked at Pierce and Jax just across the table from me. They really were good guys. I mean, they did basically save my life. What the hell would have happened if I'd been on my own and twisted my ankle? I suppose I could have crawled back to the car, but then I'd have to drive it with my left foot.

What a mess that would have been.

I'd have crashed before getting two miles down the road.

Which reminded me... I still needed to get word to Pippa. She'd surely begun to wonder where the hell I was.

"Hey guys, is there a way I can get a message to a friend at home, so she doesn't worry?"

Before anyone could answer, Blaze barged through the front door, naked and still mostly wet. He turned to face me. Who knew my little camping vacation would turn into a nude fest of some of the most gorgeous men I'd ever seen?

Maybe I could get some pictures when no one was looking. It was the only way anyone would ever believe the stories I planned to share.

"There is no way to get a message to anyone," Blaze barked, continuing through the living room.

"But Blaze, I have to let people know where I am," I called after him. "I've got friends! Work, dammit! I could get fired!"

He stopped at the doorway and turned, tilting his head, clearly annoyed. And cripes if he wasn't the biggest, most muscular man I'd ever laid eyes on. A little scary-looking actually, with that shaved head and mean-as-shit attitude.

And, despite my recent orgasm, his bad boy looks got a little purring going down in my ladybits department.

But his cock was what really got me. Sure, I was trying not to stare at the guy, but hell, he was putting it all out there for me to see. His dick was long and fat—really, really fat, like the size of my lower arm. No wonder he was grouchy. His penis was probably too long to actually fuck anybody.

"We can get a message to someone when we next go into town," he growled, his lip lifting in a sneer.

"Oh. You're going into town? Why don't you take me with you?"

Cool. Problem solved.

"We can't." He turned and walked away, his ass muscles flexing with every step he took. Like that explained everything.

Can you hate someone but still want them to fuck the stuffing out of you?

Down girl.

"Why can't I go to town?" I asked, looking between Jax and Pierce. They both stared right back at me, silent, but looking like they had something to say.

Shit, I'd had it with all their secrets. If the guys weren't going to tell me what's up, fine. I'd get my ankle healed and get the hell out. Fuck them.

Even if they were hot.

Reid came in from his bath with a towel around his waist. "Just ignore him, Jo, he's always a dick." He gave me a long, slow wink.

I wondered what it would be like with the two of them in bed—

"Leave your friend's contact info on the counter there. I'll get a message to her if I can," Blaze said, emerging from his room, barefoot. He continued buttoning up his jeans and walked into the kitchen to see what was left in the pot.

Time to be nice. More flies with honey than piss and vinegar and all. "Thanks, Blaze. That would be great. And sorry for taking so long in the tub. I didn't know baths were timed." I giggled before I could stop myself. My mom used to time my showers or else I'd stay in there all day.

"Yeah, well maybe you could think of someone other than yourself next time," Blaze spat, his mood not improving despite my attempt at being nice.

What an ass.

I jumped up as best I could and crutched over to him, getting in his face even though I only came up to his chest. "Why don't you get off my fucking back?" I hissed. "I'm not in the Army, you're not my goddamn drill sergeant, so how about you act like a normal human being, dickwad?"

The room went dead quiet. Not even Blaze had anything to say for a change. I looked around the room, and they were all pretty much looking at me with their mouths hanging open.

I then hobbled over to the sofa in the living room and propped my leg up on the coffee table. *Now*, they knew who they were dealing with. I thumbed through an old *Time* magazine. They could kiss my ass—

"Hey!"

Blaze had charged across the room and pulled me out of my seat by the arm.

"You're hurting me! Let go!" I squirmed but was no match against his strength. I popped him in the chest, where my fist thudded off rock hard muscles. "Bastard!"

The other guys stood, as if they were ready to intervene. But they didn't.

"Get up," Blaze growled. "Go to your room."

He handed me my crutch, and pointed the way. As if I didn't know.

"Are you kidding?" I asked. "Seriously, what the fuck do you think this is, a prison?"

Instead of answering, he pulled me until I nearly toppled over. But he was strong enough to keep me upright with one arm.

Of course.

"Get the fuck off me you asshole!" I screamed. "I'll go, just leave me alone."

I hobbled as fast as I could and just before I turned the corner to my room, I grabbed a huge hardback book and chucked it at him as hard as I could. It landed right on his foot, and he hollered like someone was murdering him.

What a pussy.

But I got in Pierce's room and locked the door just in time for him to pound on it.

"You'll pay for that, bitch!"

Oh. Now that didn't sound good.

I rummaged through my stuff and grabbed my handy pepper spray, not that it would stop a bull like him. But it was all I had.

"Blaze, Blaze, take it down a notch," Jax said from outside the bedroom door. "Fuck man, it was just a book."

"I'm fine dude. Hands off," Blaze said. "Who the fuck does she think she is? I mean I saw her and Pierce getting it on tonight. And wasn't she with Reid earlier? I can't keep track. Christ." I heard him storm down the hall and slam his bedroom door.

And there came a soft knock on mine.

"Jo? Hey, are you okay?" Jax asked quietly.

"Yeah. I guess," I said, hobbling over to let him in. "Sorry. I lost my head there."

He stood in the doorway, shaking his head. "That was really something. But he deserved it, in my opinion."

He entered the room and closed the door behind himself. Finally, I smiled a little. "I bet that hurt like hell, that book on Blaze's foot."

We looked at each other and smiled. I tried not to laugh, but when Jax started, it was useless. We both fell back on the bed, giggling our asses off.

"Oh my god, that was funny. I mean, Blaze didn't think it was funny, but the rest of us guys thought it was hilarious," he said, catching his breath. "You won't even believe the book you threw, either."

"What?"

He showed me the book, and even I had to laugh as the dust cover showed a foot kicking a brick. "Perfectly appropriate, you ask me."

"So you don't all hate me?" I asked.

He shook his head *no*, while trying to suppress his laugher.

Relief washed over me. I didn't know how long I was going to be stuck there, but I did know it would be way worse if *everyone* hated me. If it was just one of the four, that I could deal with.

"Nobody hates you, Jo. Not even Blaze. He's just difficult. In fact we all like you."

Oh thank god.

"Want me to show you how much?" he asked, leaning me back onto the bed.

"But what about—"

He shut me up with a deep kiss, and I had my answer.

CHAPTER 13

JAX

It made me shake my head, half in amazement, half in disbelief. Not only had Jo whacked the proverbial hornet's nest, but just when it was exploding in anger, she doubled down and whacked it again. I didn't think I'd ever seen Blaze that pissed off.

But that wasn't my problem.

Jo had tormented me with her unselfconscious sexiness since the first time I saw her skinny dipping by her campsite. Yup, I'd been out walking the perimeter as we called it, and heard a lovely female voice singing. Lo and behold, I find one of the hottest fucking women I'd ever seen with a tidy little campsite, floating in the little stream near her tent.

Without a stitch of clothing on.

Yeah, I suppose I should have just turned around and given the woman her privacy. But fuck that. Call me a peeping Tom—I hadn't seen a beautiful naked woman, except those in the porno mags we passed around the house, in way too long.

The way she emerged from the water—apple shaped tits bouncing, nice round ass jiggling, not to mention the long blonde hair clinging to her like she was freaking Lady Godiva—just about sent me over the edge.

After arriving home that first day I'd spotted her, I rubbed out three hard-ons right in a row.

When I'd been out with Pierce the next day, I'd purposely led him toward her camp in the hope that we might have the opportunity to meet her. Now she was staying at our place.

And I was kissing her. Things had a funny way of working out.

Wait till she found out what a pervy fuck I was.

Her lips were eager, maybe even a bit urgent. I understood she was frightened by Blaze's temper, and connecting physically helped temper that fear. I know it probably could have been any of us guys she relieved her stress with, and I didn't care. I planned to give her something she'd never forget.

I slipped her top over her head and her sweats down her hips, which gave me the opportunity to appreciate her smooth, lightly tanned skin with both my lips and fingers. My tongue swirled over her hard nipples, licking and sucking until I heard her breathing deepen.

I turned her over to her belly, and pulled her to her

knees, taking care to avoid her swollen ankle. "Head down," I growled, parting her legs. With her curvy ass in the air, I peeled off her lacy thong, and spread her cheeks for the view that I loved.

I'd always been an 'ass man', and what I was looking at was pure heaven. Tight, clean, delicious... and ready to feel me.

I spat on her asshole and began gently rubbing my finger over her star opening until she relaxed a bit, her breath catching as she started to push back into my massage. I'm an expert at it, knowing just how to tease, stroke, and bring a woman to the point where she wanted it.

She took longer than most, I guessed because she wasn't used to ass play, but hey, I was a patient man. Besides, looking at the prize of my efforts was more than worth taking my time.

When her puckering loosened a bit, I brought my tongue to it and she bucked her head up.

"What are you doing?" she whispered.

"Didn't I tell you to keep your head down?" I asked, pushing it back to where it belonged. "If you don't listen, you will be punished."

Her head popped back up. "What do you mean *punished*? That's the most ridiculous thing I've ever—"

"*Down*," I said, pushing her head and holding it.

"But—" she started.

Pretty girls rarely had to deal with life's consequences, and as a result, sucked at following directions.

MIKA LANE

Like keeping quiet. And not turning lights on in hidden rooms.

That's where punishment came in.

"Are you going to be quiet?" I whispered.

She tried to lift her head again, but I held it down. "What the hell—" she grumbled.

Poor Jo. She was going to have to learn the hard way.

I put my thumb in my mouth to get it nice and wet, and jammed it in her ass up to the knuckle.

She gasped, finally silent. It wasn't pain... at least, not just pain. I knew what I was doing, and there was pleasure with that pain, and a promise of more.

As I raided her ass, I reached for her clit with my other hand, where I made slow circles, showing her just how good it could be. She was getting wetter by the moment, which was a good thing, because what I planned to do needed a lot of lube.

"Oh, Jax... " she sighed.

I wiggled my thumb and she moaned, waving her butt in the air. Removing it, I rimmed her now-loosened hole, popping my tongue in and out of it in time to the strokes of my fingers on her clit. She pushed back against me, which I took as an invitation for more.

Reaching into Pierce's nightstand, I grabbed a condom, which I quickly rolled down my length, and coated it with a thick layer of the lube he had. You didn't live with a guy as long as I had with Pierce without knowing a few things about a guy. And I knew

112

that if anyone in the cabin had what I needed right at hand, it would be Pierce.

Notching my cock against her ass, I slowly pressed as she opened more. It was slow-going, but worth it.

"Push out a little bit baby. That will make it easier."

"Push out?" she murmured. "Don't do that. I don't like it."

Christ, she really was an anal virgin. I didn't know they still existed except in storybooks or under the age of nineteen.

"Have you ever done this, baby? Been fucked in the butt?"

"No. I don't think I like it. It feels weird."

I pressed a little harder, and despite her protests, she pushed out, allowing the fattest part of my head in. She groaned with pleasure.

"How do you know you don't like it if you've never done it?" I asked pushing my entire head in.

I knew I was doing something right when she started making guttural, grunting noises. Her breath caught again and again, and she pushed back while one of her hands flew to her clit, massaging furiously. Smart girl. That would help her relax.

I drizzled some lube around her ass, and began rocking myself in and out. Fuck, I don't think I'd ever been so hard, and all I could think about was exploding in her bum. But first I was going to make sure she came so hard she'd beg for my cock in her ass every day of her life.

She probably had no idea she could come from ass sex.

But she was going to learn.

I leaned toward her head, burying my dick almost to the hilt. "You good, baby? You like me in your tight ass? It doesn't hurt too much?"

Instead of answering, she pushed back against me, almost smacking my balls. Her hand continued to work her clit, and she suddenly tightened on my dick.

Her back arched and she pounded her free hand on the bed.

"Jax, I'm coming... I'm coming, oh god..." she rasped hoarsely. "Fuck me more."

Well, that was all I needed. I unleashed myself on her, thrusting in and out with deep, long strokes that left both of us moaning in seconds. I wanted to draw it out, but her ass was so tight, so perfect, that I was trembling on the edge even before I could count to ten.

It didn't matter. Jo's moans rose again, and when she tightened around my cock, her voice lost to anything but gibbering cries of pleasure, I knew she was coming.

I let myself go, and moments later my dick lengthened and I pushed my hips against her ass, pumping my sperm while she clenched me nearly to the point of pain.

We caught our breaths as I wrapped my arms and legs around her, something I'd been dying to do since I'd first laid eyes on her.

"I've never done that before," she murmured, subdued.

Fuck, was I getting hard again? "I know. I could tell."

She sighed. Just like I knew she would.

"You liked it," I continued.

"Maybe." She snuggled into me, probably a little embarrassed to admit to liking something so crude, so base. Maybe even borderline immoral.

"It's okay… as long as it's good, it's okay."

I buried my nose in her hair, and smelled the wood fire used to heat the tub. Clean, outdoorsy, and slightly of the bio soap we all used. Nothing perfume-y about it. Nothing civilized about it. All good.

Yes, I was hard again, dammit.

She turned her head toward me. "Hey I noticed you with a guitar," she said softly.

"Yeah, I play a little. Not very well."

"I write music," she said, smiling as she wiggled her hips. "Maybe not very well, either."

"Get out of here. Are you kidding?" Cripes, was I going to fall for this one.

"I'm not kidding. I'd love to show you some of my stuff. I've been saving to get a demo tape together."

"Whoa. That's expensive. Hiring musicians and all."

"Don't I know it," she said, resigned.

"Hey, I have a question for you. Why were you camping all by yourself?" I asked.

She flipped over to face me fully, her blonde hair splayed over the pillows. "Why are you up here in the cabin?"

Touché.

Okay. Time to share. "Well, it was Pierce's family's cabin. He inherited it and invited me to come to live here after the accident, when I lost my shit."

She stiffened. "Accident? What accident?"

I took a deep breath. Of course she didn't know. How could she? After several years, the words still caught in my throat. "My wife and baby daughter were killed in a car accident."

She gasped. "Oh god."

"Yeah. Pierce saw the shape I was in and brought me up here. Now I can't imagine living anywhere else."

She intertwined her fingers with mine and in that moment we were close in a way that I felt in my soul. Corny shit, I know, but it was like our hearts were touching. Had we really only just met?

Dude, no falling in love. Just no.

"I'm so sorry. Good lord." She dabbed her eyes with a corner of the sheet.

I said nothing. There was really nothing to say about such a tragedy.

"It's good you had a place to retreat to."

Her compassion was getting to me, and I needed to change the subject. "You are right. And I love it up here."

"So what's all the secrecy about? With you guys living up here?" she asked.

Christ, she didn't give up. "You gotta stop asking that stuff. Nothing good will come of it. We all have our reasons, and some are darker than others. But living off the grid is freaking awesome. Don't think I've ever been happier."

"But don't you miss women?" she asked. "Or are Pierce's toys for... other reasons?"

Christ, this girl and her questions. I laughed lightly.

"Of course I do. That's why I was watching you skinny dip in your campsite. And you'll have to ask Pierce about his toys."

Her head popped off the pillow. "Oh my god. You fucking perv."

"Yeah, whatever. Now you tell me what the hell *you're* doing up here."

CHAPTER 14

JOELLE

I really didn't know what to say. I mean, Jax had watched me skinny dip like a damn Peeping Tom. Probably even watched me play with my vibrator on that warm rock where I'd sunned myself. But I couldn't really say anything. Hell, I'd watched him and Pierce bathing.

Guess I was just as bad.

Or horny.

I looked away from him. I was a shitty liar, and if he couldn't see my eyes, maybe he'd buy my B.S.

"I… I just wanted to get away. You know how it is."

I glanced at his skeptical face. Dammit.

"Why don't you believe me?" I asked.

He rolled his eyes, giving up. "So back to music," he said, as if everything was cool.

Once again there were no answers about life on

Savage Mountain from him, so he wasn't getting any from me about my travels. But I wasn't giving up. If you can't kick in the door... find a window. At least, that's what I'd heard somewhere.

"Yes, music. I'd love to hear you play."

He air guitared with excitement, so endearing I couldn't help but catch some feels for him just for that instant. "That would be awesome. I could try out some of your music. Can you sing? We could jam together."

Now that made me laugh.

"I don't know about jamming. I'm a terrible singer," I said honestly. Once he heard me sing, he'd never ask again, that was for sure. "I'm pretty much a tune in a bucket sort of gal."

"I'll teach you," he insisted.

I had to laugh at that. "Okay. I accept the challenge."

Coyotes started to howl and bark, this time right outside the house. I squeaked, and threw myself into his arms, worried.

"Hey, don't be afraid," Jax said, snuggling into me. "They're just... well, being coyotes."

"Oh, they just startled me. You have to admit, that sound is something to get used to. They sound like a dog that has just been hit by a car. Not exactly sooth- ing. But I need to go to the bathroom, and I can't go out there now, not with those critters so nearby."

"Oh, they won't bother you." Jax chuckled. "They'd be scared of you."

"Easy for you to say," I said. "You're big enough to

take on a whole pack with a butter knife and walk out unscathed."

He sat up. "I'll tell you what. I'll go with you. You probably need help, anyway. I don't want you falling flat on your face because of that crutch."

"Really? Oh, thank you." I swung my feet off the bed and began to pull on my sweats while Jax pulled on his jeans and fleece, covering up his fine physique and dramatic tattoos.

He held his arm to help me up. Who would have thought such a sweetheart would also be into kinky butt sex?

The minute we opened the cabin front door, all animal sounds ceased. Guess it wasn't hard to scare off the little buggers, after all.

"Hey, will you spend the night with me? Like sleep with me?" I asked suddenly. "You know... for warmth?"

He smiled and laid a juicy one on my lips. "'Course. I was planning on it."

Something startled me awake, and I quickly realized it was a *skritch-skritch* in the walls. Jax was gone and the sun was seeping through the shutters into the room.

The sound was coming from the direction of the closet, the one for accessing the hidden room.

Oh my god. What other secrets could this house have? Fuck. Reaching for the pepper spray...

But then it scooted up the wall and across the ceiling. Okay. Not a person, but still discomforting knowing some sort of woodland creature considered the house his own. Came with the territory, I supposed, like the coyotes and the big-assed spider I'd seen hanging out in the latrine.

Rustic living wasn't for me. That's all there was to it. And my camping days were over. My one and only trip had been sufficient. Didn't need to repeat that shit.

I hobbled out to the living room and kitchen, which was dead silent. No sign of the guys, and the only sound to be heard was the singing of the birds, which was actually really nice.

Where the hell was everybody? It's not like they had to get to the office or some such. Had they gone into town without me? Or deserted me? Left me here to rot?

I spied a note on the counter, and picked it up.

Jo... had to get some chores done. Breakfast and lunch are on the stove. Relax, enjoy some books, and we'll be back this afternoon.

The signature at the bottom from Jax made me chuckle, and I folded the note before thinking what I was going to do for the day.

So I guess they weren't trying to kill me off that particular day, as much as Blaze might like to.

I poured myself a cup of still-warm coffee from the insulated carafe they must have brought from civilization, and sat down to eat a hard-boiled egg and a chunk of freshly made bread. While they might not have had much variety in their diets, what they did have was pretty good.

I supposed I could even get used to venison, given enough time.

But who was I kidding? I was out of there the first chance I got. Damn right.

The other good news was, my ankle hurt less, and while the swelling had gone down slightly, it was now bruised like a ripe plum. But I knew that was all good, and that it was healing, slowly but surely.

I shifted again as my ass protested lightly over Jax's pummeling. What the hell had I been thinking, to let him do that?

Although it had been fucking hot. And dirty.

God, what was I turning into?

I'd only just been with Reid and Pierce.

That left Blaze, but that would never happen. One, the guy fucking hated me, and two, I'd gotten a look at his dick, and he was coming nowhere near me with that monster.

No sir.

Since I was in the house alone, I decided to jump on the unexpected opportunity to snoop. Because, why not? I was blown away by all the books in the living room, which upon closer inspection ranged from several of my favorite romances and mysteries, to histories of the big world wars, to economics texts.

What an odd range of reading materials. I mean, Dostoevsky right next to Jackie Collins?

I hobbled back to my room, thinking I might try

again to see if I could get a cell signal. I couldn't be sure the guys would actually let Pippa know I was alive and well.

By this point though, I was probably fired from my job—not that I cared that much, seeing as I hated the place.

But I did want Pippa to know where the hell I was, and that I hadn't been eaten by a bear. I had no doubt she was crazy with worry and I felt horrible about that.

Where the hell was my phone? I bumped around the house wondering where I'd left it. Strange, I could have sworn I put it back in my pack after my last attempt to start it up, when Blaze had screamed at me in the closet.

Ah, there it was, in the living room. I must have abandoned it there the night before when Blaze had dragged me around by the arm. The nerve of that asshole, threatening me. I hoped his foot had a painful bruise from where the book I'd thrown had landed on it.

I flicked the phone *on*, but of course there was no signal. Why did I even keep checking? It was like when you were looking for something to eat. You opened the fridge five times, as if something tasty would have somehow magically appeared since the last time you checked.

Guess there's always hope.

I figured I'd get some fresh air and headed out to check the water in the hot tub. I knew the thing was really for bathing, but it really had felt good to soak under the stars, and if I could sneak a little more time in it when no one was around, that would be amazing. But when I got there, not only was the fire out, but the water had been drained, leaving only little puddles in the bottom of the tub's liner.

Probably for the best—after five people had bathed in it.

And since I didn't know how to refill the thing, or how to start a fire in the heater element, that ended that idea almost as fast as I came up with it.

Instead, I circled the house, something I'd not done to that point, mainly because I'd felt compelled to stay in my room. Well, Pierce's room.

The house really was charming, built like a traditional log cabin, the kind you see in the movies, with pine needles sprinkled over the steep roof, and long eaves protecting the old, wavy glass windows.

I was quiet with my hobbling, dead silent in fact. If anyone was coming back to the house, I wanted to hear them before they heard me. Getting yelled at was getting old.

The landscape was cleared in probably a twenty-foot radius around the house, I presumed as a sort of firebreak. But at the edge of the clearing the woods rose up, thick, dark, and intimidating. It wouldn't do to get lost out there, not at all.

I continued crutching around the property when something unusual caught my eye.

Right at the edge of the clearing, where the trees started, I found a discrete row of barbed wire woven among the trees. I followed it for a bit, and found it extended the entire circumference of the property.

Was it attached to some sort of alarm system? And if so, how would that work without electricity?

The second odd thing I encountered was what I guessed would be called a cellar door. It was level with the ground, its corners and sides overgrown with weeds. I wouldn't have noticed it if I hadn't stepped right on it. The brittle wood cracked under my good foot, and I hopped off the thing as fast as I could. I didn't need to end up in a hole in the ground, and get in trouble with Blaze for another indiscretion.

But curiosity got the better of me, and after painfully kneeling down, I pulled on the doors' handles. Not surprisingly, they didn't budge. I pressed on the old wood to see if it would give way, but after that first crackle, it didn't move. Maybe it was reinforced on the other side.

I reminded myself that I really ought to be minding my own business, and worked my way around to the front porch to relax and put my foot up. At the far end was the swing where I'd gotten it on with Pierce and where I'd left the hiking boot I'd been wearing on my good foot.

Surprised Blaze didn't try to hit me over the head with it.

I leaned back in an old rocking chair and propped both my feet up on the porch railing. Dragonflies whizzed by looking for mates, and the crickets started up again once I'd stopped moving around. I could see why the guys liked being up there, with the peace and the sweet-smelling air.

And despite the rough nature of things, I wondered if I could get used to it. All the nature, not to mention testosterone of four hot as hell alpha dudes, got my motor revving. With no one around, I moved my hand between my legs and started a little rubbing.

Christ, I must have been going through a hormonal tidal wave... I'd never been so constantly horny. Well, fuck it. I was going to have fun while I could, when I could.

Before I could really get warmed up, I heard the loud crackling of wood, as if a tree were falling down, followed by a large *thump*, presumably as it hit the ground. I grabbed my crutch and made my way toward the noise. I know curiosity killed the cat, and if it shortened my life, it was a risk that was worth it.

I followed a path I'd not noticed before, taking careful note of my surroundings so I could find my way back. I hobbled along for what seemed an eternity, and finally stopped to rest, perspiration running down the sides of my face. Who knew using a crutch would require so much energy?

As I rested, I listened to the voices in the distance, much the way I had when the guys had happened upon my campsite. And just as I had then, I moved behind a tree until I could suss out the situation.

The voices were those of Jax and Reid, and just hearing them made my heart pound. I looked down and found my nipples hard as little rocks, and there was a spreading warmth between my legs. It was no surprise really, my Pavlov's dog-type reaction to them.

I strained to hear their conversation, and resigned myself to moving closer.

I could finally see them, shirtless and covered in perspiration as they were chopping up the tree I'd heard fall. Over and over, they raised their axes and brought them down, splitting the hard wood like it was made of nothing but air. Their backs flexed as they moved in a striking dance that I wished I could have caught on film.

Seriously, they were beautiful.

"Wonder what Pierce and Blaze are gonna bring back. That venison we had last night was killer," Jax said. "Good seasoning."

Glad *he* liked it.

Reid rested his axe on the ground, and leaned on the handle while he brushed sweat from his brow with the back of his hand. "Well, they're good hunters so I'm expecting something special. Although I did put in an order for wild boar. I could really go for some kind of pork."

Crack. Another log split like it was a little Tinkertoy.

Jax picked up a chunk of branch about as big around as his arm and tossed it into a big wheelbarrow. "I think we're getting close to done. We've chopped enough to fill the cart and bring it up to the house. And we'll need the saw to break up the main trunk."

"Cool. I'm ready for a break. Hey, where's the

water?" Reid asked, looking around. "Shit, did we bury it in the wood again?"

I ducked behind a tree before he saw me.

Jax wiped the sweat off his face too, and squinted up at the sun. "Shoulda worn a cap."

"She's really something isn't she?"

Holy shit. What a conversation to stumble upon.

"Fuck man, you're not lying there. She's so hot. And feisty. I like that. A lot," Reid said. "Listen man... you cool about what she and I got up to?"

"As long as you're cool with what she and I got up to," Jax said with a chuckle. "You know, I hope she's around for awhile, although that's probably not what Blaze wants."

"I know. But on the other hand, I'm not sure he wants to let her go. I'm not sure he's *going* to let her go."

"I know what you mean."

"Cripes, wait till she finds that out. Ain't gonna be pretty," he added. "That'll be fun to watch, actually."

What the fuck? Keep me? At the cabin? What could they possibly want me there for? I had pretty much nothing to contribute. Oh wait...

Nope, I decide when, where, and with whom. I burst out of the woods toward the guys. They weren't keeping me anywhere, I didn't give a damn how hot any of them were.

CHAPTER 15

REID

Next time we drew lots to see who had to get firewood and who was going hunting, I was really going to put my foot down. The last three times we'd done so, I'd been stuck with the goddamn chopping.

I was beginning to wonder if the straws we pulled were rigged or something.

Not that hunting wasn't hard but c'mon, chopping wood was some seriously shitty grunt work. I don't care how sharp our axes were, or how good we got at it, taking down a two foot thick pine was a pain in the ass, even if it was full of dry rot.

It was damn hot under the sun, and while we'd started work in the very early morning, it was no longer cool enough to keep on with the hard labor we were performing. The calluses on my palms were starting to burn, a sign that blisters were on their way.

I was ready to call it quits for the day.

"Hey, maybe next time someone goes into town, they can get us some gloves for work like this," I said.

"Seriously, even some of those military gloves you guys used to have would be nice."

Jax nodded. "Oh man, that's a smart idea—"

"Excuse me, did someone say something about going into town? I'd like to be on that bus when it leaves."

Jo emerged from the woods like an apparition, her crutch stumping on the pine needles like a manic pirate or something. Honestly, it startled the crap out of Jax and me. There she stood, with her blonde hair partially pinned up, the rest sexily spilling all over her shoulders, in short shorts and a snug little tank top. One foot was nearly all white, clad in a sneaker, while the swollen one was bare and bright purple.

One look and I couldn't wait to lick her pussy again. And possibly more...

"Well, hello. Where'd you come from, pretty girl?" Jax said, a relaxed grin fixed on his face.

Yeah, Jax was whipped. Actually I had to admit we all were. I mean, he and I had just completed a conversation where we admitted to both having sex with the girl, and neither of us being upset with the other. I bet Pierce was the same way.

Well, maybe not Blaze. But give him time. I knew he liked a pretty girl, and in particular one who didn't put up with his shit. He was not immune, much as he might pretend to be. If Jo kept standing up to him, she was going to have him wrapped around her little finger before the end of the week.

"Hi guys," Jo said, flirtatiously. "I was just out for some exercise."

Bullshit. No one with a sprained ankle on a crutch exercised by walking that far. And her eyes were too angry to just be playfully out for a lark.

She'd overheard us.

"Really, Jo?" I asked, trying to give her an out. "Sure you weren't looking for us?"

Her eyes widened, and her voice was too innocent to be believable. "Nope. No, just out for a walk."

It was clear she was full of shit, but what could she have been up to? It's not like she could walk off the damn mountain. It must have taken her forever to cover the little bit of ground that she had.

"You shouldn't have left the house with your ankle like that, Jo," Jax said, concerned. "What if you had fallen? Or gotten lost?"

She shrugged. "I suppose you're right. But all is well. Anyway, what were you guys talking about? Going into town or something? I saw the note, and just wondered."

What was she up to? She might have been gorgeous, but she was also sneaky. There's calling Blaze on his shit, and then there's trying to CIA us. Even I didn't like that.

"Not sure what we were talking about," I said, looking at Jax who also nodded slightly. "We do occasionally take trips to town, maybe once a month or so."

She inched up to us, and sat down on a piece of the big tree we'd just felled. "When are you going next time? Maybe I could go with."

I looked at Jax, who shrugged. "You never know," I said, even though Blaze had shot down the idea just the night before.

"True... so, how much wood do you have to chop down?" she asked, changing subjects quickly.

It was hard to stay on balance with Jo, but I knew she was trying to keep us off balance. Still, I couldn't be mad—I would have done the same thing in her situation.

"We're always chopping wood. We can't let ourselves run out. That would be a big problem." I had quickly moved past wondering what the hell she was doing there, to thinking how I might get her clothes off. After all, there she was, the sun was nice, and my body was warm...

"Why don't you do something for us, Jo? I mean, since we're putting you up and all?" I teased.

She rolled her eyes like the sassy pain in the ass that she was. "Are you serious, Reid? You bring me to your house because I'm injured, then essentially tell me that I *owe* you guys?" She stood and put her hands on her hips.

"Well, what is it you want?"

Yeah, like she didn't know what was coming.

"Why don't you come over here and kiss me, baby?"

Jax asked. "I mean, we did just get the wood for your bath tonight."

She looked at him for a moment, then shrugged and made her way over to him. Despite her movements being anything but graceful, she was still somehow sexy as hell.

She positioned herself right in front of Jax, and arched into him as he scooped an arm around her waist, pulling her closer. From where I stood, I could admire the little shorts that were so tight on her bum, her cheeks perfectly outlined.

Jax looked past her at me, and nodded, then pressed her lips to his. So he was as down with the idea as I was. Good... I was going to enjoy it, then.

As she sank into him, I approached her from behind, pulling her hair off her neck and running my lips along her silky skin. Her head dropped back and she moaned lightly. I reached around her and pushed my hands down the front of her shorts, where I quickly found her bare pussy.

"Your fingers feel nice, Reid," she murmured.

Jax, in the meantime, had lifted her shirt up to her neck, and was going to town on her delectable tits.

She pushed her ass back into my now-raging cock and I ground it between her cheeks. God, Jax had been here? Lucky bastard... I'd never even thought it possible.

"Hey," Jax said, "come sit over here." He took her by the hand.

I pulled my hands out of Jo's shorts and Jax and I

helped her over to the pile of wood we'd been stacking, and helped her sit. Then he looked at me.

"Think this lady can handle two cocks at once?" he asked. "What do you think, Jo?"

I liked the way my friend thought.

Jo, on the other hand, sat there with her eyes wide open. And pretty soon her mouth would be wide open, too.

When our trousers were down around our ankles, we each held our hard dicks for her to taste. She didn't hesitate.

She put a hand on each one of us, and brought Jax to her lips. She ran her tongue around his head and under the rim, stroking his balls in the process. Then she took his length into her mouth.

All the way into her mouth. Damn… this girl was skilled in ways I didn't think were possible.

Jax and I looked at each other.

"Holy shit, bro," I said, watching his dick disappear down her throat. It was sexy as fuck, and I swallowed, my cock jumping in her grip.

"Oh, damn… " Jax rasped, his head dropping back, his hands on his hips for balance. "Fucking perfect. What an angel…."

She let him go, and turned to me with saliva dribbling down her chin and onto her chest. With one hand on my cock, she lifted it up and out of the way, and began to devour my balls.

"Holy shit," I murmured, spreading my legs to increase her access. "Suck me, girl," I said as her tongue lapped me. "Take all of me."

On command, she moved to my dick, and when I opened my eyes I saw Jax between her legs, shimmying her shorts off her lovely hips. In about two seconds, his face was buried between her legs and he was lapping at her lovely pussy while stroking himself.

"Goddamn, baby, you taste good," he murmured to her.

She just moaned in response, seeing as her mouth was full to the brim.

"Yeah, baby," Jax continued, "come for me. In my mouth." The faster he worked her over, the harder she sucked me.

There she was, beneath the two of us, beautiful and delicate, small in relation to the mass of our bodies. And yet she wielded such power, power she probably didn't even know she had.

Or did she? She couldn't have stumbled upon us that afternoon completely by accident. But I would think that through later. With my cock deep in her throat, now was not the time. I thrust forward to get deeper in her mouth, and her gagging sounds were about the hottest fucking thing I'd ever heard.

She released me from her mouth, and looked up at me while Jax lapped at her pussy.

"Is anybody gonna fuck me? Please?" she asked, with a pout. "I've had cocks in my mouth, in my ass... but none in my pussy. Please?"

Jax looked up from his position between her legs, palming the head of his dick and jerking himself faster.

"Stand up," he growled at her. "You're gonna get two this time."

I pulled her to standing and helped her balance on her one good foot. Turning her away from us, I bent her forward, lifting her sore ankle so it rested on a convenient log.

"I don't suppose you have a condom?"

She shook her head.

"I'll pull out."

She nodded, and I notched myself at her opening, nice and juicy thanks to Jax, and thrust deep into her, tipping her forward, and over the woodpile in front of us. Doubled over, she held onto the logs and turned her head to take Jax into her mouth.

We double-teamed her brutally until I pulled out and came all over her back, just in time to see Jax exploding on her face. Stunned, he and I stepped back, holding our cocks, and watched her limp, bent, and open, covered in our cum.

She lifted her head from the woodpile. "Amazing... so good," she murmured, grinning. "And yet...."

"What?" I asked, and she smiled wider.

"I want even more. You have me hooked, damn you."

The feeling was mutual.

CHAPTER 16

JOELLE

Afterwards, the guys helped me dress before they put me in some sort of wheelbarrow thing they used for transporting wood so I wouldn't have to walk back to the cabin.

Not that I would have been able to, anyway.

I'd had a drunken three-some once before, a long time ago in college. It had basically sucked because neither guy knew what the hell he was doing. The just lined up to take turns.

I never knew what all the fuss was, with the *ménages* my friends bragged about.

So I'd never considered it again, and chalked it up to college experimentation. Like that time I kissed a girl and played with her tits after a few Jagermeister shots. I wasn't remotely lesbian, and I proved it to myself that night.

But in the threesome category, I'd just struck gold. Seriously.

After Jax and Reid had turned me into their cum slut, and painted me in their spunk, I was immobile, bent over a pile of wood, scraped and splintered by the rough bark. I had small scratches on my knees, chest, and hands, which bore the brunt of the punishment they'd meted out to me.

And I'd never felt better.

The cart I was riding in bumped and jostled against the uneven ground, sending my butt rolling from side to side. The guys, however, had devised a shock absorber of sorts to make sure my swollen ankle did not get any more abused than necessary.

We were quiet on the trek back to the house, all three us not only sated but frankly, amazed by our zesty session in the great outdoors. I didn't know about those two, but it had been epic for me.

As we got closer to the house, we saw that Pierce and Blaze had returned from their hunting trip, or wherever it was that they went. Using my handy crutch, I propelled myself out of the cart, and headed right for him. I held my head up bravely, even though the night before he'd claimed he wanted to kill me.

"Blaze, are you going into town any time soon? I really need to get a message to my friend Pippa. She's going to be worried sick. Maybe even call the authorities. On second thought, she'll definitely call the authorities. I don't know what they'll do, but if I can just let her know I'm safe, that will save everyone a lot of trouble."

He looked directly at me for the first time since, well, I'd arrived. His green eyes glittered in a way I hadn't noticed, their elegance a sharp contrast to his shaved head and angled jaw. Even though I was a tall woman at five foot eight, he still peered straight down at me when he spoke.

"We have no plans to go to town."

He said it like he was the Pharaoh or something, like in those old movies. *So let it be written, so let it be done*, and all that shit.

But I didn't like being brushed off and was ready to give him a piece of my mind when I remembered what had happened the night before, with him grabbing me by the arm.

I looked around at the rest of the guys to gauge their reactions, but they were giving nothing away aside from glancing at each other.

C'mon, I wanted to say. *I've fucked three of you. Can't you level with me?*

But of course, I didn't. I already had enough problems, and antagonizing the guys was certainly not going to help matters. I'd had sex, not gotten them to pledge their loyalty to me like I was some sort of mountaintop queen.

So I excused myself to take a rest before dinner. I was dying to have a little soak in the hot tub, but I wasn't sure they fired it up every night, and I didn't want to look like an idiot by asking. If I had to wait another day for a hot bath, I could certainly survive that. In the meantime, I could give myself a little sponge bath at the pump outside, like I'd seen Reid doing when we returned from chopping wood.

The fact of the matter was, if Pippa did indeed alert the authorities about my being missing, and directed them to my car and campsite because she knew both locations, wouldn't they eventually find me here, at the cabin?

And if the guys really had something to hide, then that could mean trouble for everyone.

"Have a good rest," Pierce said.

I stretched, yawning dramatically. "Thanks."

I went to my room and quietly flipped the lock. Time for some sleuthing. I had to find out what was up these guys' asses, and see if I could get through to Pippa somehow.

Grabbing my flashlight, I went into the closet containing the hidden door and entered the room where I had been holed up the previous day when I'd gotten into so much trouble. It was clear there was more than met the eye to that damn place, and to protect myself, I needed to get to the bottom of it.

Once inside the room where I'd cooled my heels when god knows what was going on in the house, I pressed my ear against the other door that led to yet another secret room. It was locked. Of course. Turning back to the main room, I rummaged in the old desk for something to force the lock open.

A long, skinny letter opener looked like just the thing.

After a little twisting, and a lot of sweating, the lock turned with a squeak. I froze to see if my noise had alerted anyone in the house, but heard no approaching footsteps.

So far, so good.

Cripes, if these guys were hiding something, what the hell were they doing with such a lame lock on the door? I mean, if I could get it open, anybody surely could.

I pushed the door slowly, not sure what I'd find on the other side, and shone my flashlight around the room. Now it was *my* turn to make some noise.

But I didn't. I'd placed my hand over my mouth.

It was pitch dark, save for my flashlight, and smelled like an old basement. Must and mold filled my every breath, and a piece of metal fence caught my eye. When I got closer I could see it formed a sort of cage held shut with a padlock. Inside was a huge cache of weapons—small guns, big guns, guns that look like they would kill a ton of people in a matter of seconds.

These guys were ready for some serious shit.

What would anybody do with all those guns?

I moved around the dank room and came upon a clothes rack. I poked through the scratchy garments to find they were military uniforms—what kind, I couldn't tell, but they were definitely uniforms of some sort.

And there were computers. Slim, powerful looking laptops, on desks, connected to electricity.

Electricity? What in the fucking fuck?

Where were they getting that from?

Jesus, I should have just stayed at home in Vegas. I never should have come to Savage Mountain, and never should have tried to prove to the world what a badass camper I was, because I was really just a waitress in a shitty restaurant on the Vegas strip.

I craned my neck back toward the bedroom again—sure, I'd locked the door but whatever it was these guys did, I'd think getting into my bedroom wouldn't be much of a challenge.

The coast was clear. So far.

I sat at one of the computers and wiggled the mouse to see what would happen. The screen lit right up. However, it asked me for a password. Crap.

But if there was some way I could get a browser open—like a guest browser—and bypass the password requirement, I might be able to send a message to someone. I clicked around and when I made no progress with the first computer I'd tried, I moved on to the next one. I didn't know much about computers, but it was worth trying.

Shit. No luck. Computers right there at my literal fingertips, and they'd do me no good.

Goddammit.

I was fucked.

And when I felt a hard tug on my hair, I knew I was royally fucked.

CHAPTER 17

BLAZE

I should have known the little bitch wasn't capable of minding her own business. And now her nosiness put all our lives in danger.

Help someone out, give them a free place to stay, and this is what you get.

Fuck that.

I learned not to help people a long time ago. I wish the rest of the guys in the house subscribed to the same policy. All I'd demanded was that she not poke her nose where it didn't belong, and now... now the shit had hit the fan.

I could have broken her neck with the grip I had on her long hair. But, as furious as I was, hers was not a murderable offense. Although another prank like this might be, and she seemed to be pretty goddamn good at pushing her luck.

"Get up," I growled.

She screamed in surprise, her hands flying to mine to try and pry them out of her hair. But she had no leverage, nor any strength compared to mine. I had her tilted backwards in her chair, and besides, she had only one leg she could really use.

"Get off me motherfucker!" she screamed. "What do you have going on in here? What is all this shit?"

I put my face close to hers, so close I could feel her panting, frightened breath. "I have killed for less than this. So *shut up*." I yanked her hair to subdue her stubborn ass.

Dragging her out of the control room, I propelled her back to Pierce's room. Pinning her against the wall, I got right in her face.

"We let you stay here, and this is how you repay us? You go through our things? Pry into our private lives?"

I took several deep breaths. I couldn't remember the last time I was so close to losing my shit. Actually, I did remember. And it hadn't ended well for the person on the other end.

She narrowed her eyes and pressed her lips together hard. She was not going to back down easily. But if she wanted to live, never mind crash at my home until she could walk the fuck off the mountain, she was going to have to make some changes. Some big changes.

And she was going to have to learn that real fast.

"Get off me," she hissed, squirming against my

hands, which pinned her arms against the wall, over her head. "I deserve to know what's going on here!"

Christ, had there ever been a more naive, or entitled person, on the face of the earth?

But she clearly thought she was smarter than me because her next step, predictably, was to try to knee me in the balls. Too bad for her I knew the move and already had my hips shifted. Her thigh hadn't lifted more than a few inches when it met mine and I pressed my body tighter against hers.

She had no hope.

Dumbass. Who did she think she was dealing with?

Her face contorted with red anger, like a pissed off cat. "Motherfucker!"

I hissed back at her, so close my lips nearly touched her face. "You are an ungrateful bitch. After all we've done for you."

"I did nothing wrong," she hissed. "I got hurt, get carried up here to find you four acting like... fucking psychopaths, honestly. I get yelled at, lied to, grabbed, yanked, pulled... you can't blame me for wanting to know what goes on in this place. It's called survival." She continued trying to wrestle out of my arms. Christ, she was persistent.

"Your snooping is not survival. It's suicidal. You've just crossed a line that you will not be able to return from."

She screwed up her face at me. "What the hell does that mean?"

"Godammit, you just won't quit, will you?" I

growled. "Well, I guess the only way to shut you up is like what Jax said… you're gonna get the whole five dollar fucking tour. Now I'm going to let go of you, and I want you to go over to the bed."

I slowly released her arms and then backed her off the wall. Of course, she made a dash for the door, which was pretty much futile because how fast can you move on one foot?

"All right. I'm done with this bullshit. No more chances," I said, picking her up by the waist and carrying her over to the bed. Her arms and legs flailed, but really, she was just wasting her energy and mine. Little fool.

I threw her down on the bed, and pulled some zip ties out of my pocket. I'd really hoped I wouldn't have to use them. But she had given me no choice.

I straddled her middle and tied her hands to the bedframe above her head.

"Let me go, you psycho. You'll pay for this."

Reid slowly walked into the room. "Hey Blaze, do you really think this is necessary—"

"GET OUT," I growled without turning around. "And shut the door."

He slammed the bedroom door hard behind himself to express his obvious displeasure. I'd deal with him and his soft-heartedness later. His tendencies were exactly what would get us in trouble, and be the ruin of our safe haven.

I didn't care how hot she was, or how great of a dick she sucked.

She wasn't worth it. No one was. *Nothing* was.

The kicking subsided, and her protests were reduced to rolling eyes and trying to get comfortable under my weight.

I remained on top of her and intended to do so until we'd reached some sort of understanding.

"I'm not hurting you, am I?" I asked, not sure why I was asking. It wasn't like I was going to change anything I was doing.

She bit her lip, looking at me like she had to decide how to answer. "No, this is totally comfortable, being tied to a bed with a man twice my size, who is getting his rocks off by pinning me down. I've heard a lot of guys have this fantasy."

Oh, mental games now? If I didn't kill her, I swore I was going to end up marrying this bitch. "You're fine. We need to talk, and now that I've got your attention—"

A strange smirk crossed her face.

"You think this is funny?" I asked.

She took a deep, annoyed breath. "Okay. Let me lay it out for you. What the fuck? You guys are nothing more than grown up Boy Scouts. Get over yourselves. You want to know what a person with *balls* does? She gets up every day, puts on a cheesy maid costume, and waits on disgusting, ugly men whose pastime is drooling over women, and scarfing down bad chicken fingers and *nachos con queso* for a cheap lunch!"

Why wasn't I surprised that's what she did for work? And while I was sorry she led such a shitty life, to be honest, it just wasn't my problem. Protecting the cabin was, however.

"All right. Time to teach you a lesson," I said, releasing one of her ties, and flipping her over onto her stomach.

I yanked her shorts down below her ass, followed by her lacy panties.

"Stop it," she screamed. "What the hell do you think you're doing?"

Whack. I smacked her bottom so hard my palm stung. That meant her ass stung but good.

"Ouch, *whatthefuckdoyouthinkyou'redoing* you psycho motherfucker?" she howled, squirming as if she could get away.

"Count them," I said. "That was one."

"Fuck you!"

Whack.

She screamed.

"They're not going to stop until you start counting. I've got all day, how 'bout you? A bruised ass is not going to feel too good."

I raised my hand, poised for the next strike.

"One," she whispered.

"That was two."

"Okay! *Two!*" she yelled.

Whack.

Silence.

"I don't hear anything," I said quietly.

"Three."

Whack.

"Four."

And on we went until we'd reached nearly twenty. Her ass was hot to the touch, a bright, angry red. She was gripping the sheets with her free hand, breathing deeply to the point of panting.

I smoothed my hands over her fevered bum, watching her slowly released the purchase she had on the bed. Leaning closer, I found her face damp with tears, despite her calm expression.

I moved off my straddle, and cut the last of the zip ties holding her to the bed. I pulled her to me and she crumpled into my arms, her head burrowing in my chest. Wrapping her in one of the blankets from the bed, I scooped her up.

Her arms fell around me, and she sniffled lightly.

I brought her to my room.

Gently placing her on my bed, I undressed her and pulled the covers up. I lit a candle, its light dancing across my walls and over the ceiling.

I lay on the bed next to her, on my side, to see her.

"Hey."

"You jerk," she said, weakly trying to punch me.

And as before, I caught her wrist in a tight grip, at which she gasped in pain.

"Hey. I'm not the bastard you think I am," I said.

"You hate me. I know it," she sobbed, mumbling to herself. "Fucking asshole, it's not my fault."

Before I could ask what she meant, there was a knock on my bedroom door.

"Everything okay in there?" Pierce asked.

I looked at Jo, wanting to hear her response.

The knock came again.

"We're fine. Thank you for checking," she called out, then sniffled. "Thanks, Pierce!"

She gazed up at me from under her dark, wet lashes and before I had another thought, my mouth was on hers with a desire I didn't think I still possessed. All my anger channeled into a base need—and what I needed was *her*.

I threw the blankets to the floor and stripped off my clothes, rubbing my aching cock against her leg while I ravished her pretty mouth. I wanted those lips on my pulsing shaft, but there was time for that yet. I put a thumb into her mouth and eased it open, her vulnerability rushing over me in a wave of passion that made my throat tighten.

How could she do this to me? In one instant, she pried at my anger with her unflinching confrontation. She fought me at every turn. Then she pierced past all my defenses with a simple parting of her lips, and a tongue stroking my thumb.

I parted her legs, and found her wet and ready, as I knew she'd be from the spanking. I placed her legs over my shoulders and lifted her hips several inches off the bed. I sheathed myself with a condom I'd grabbed from Pierce's nightstand, and pressed into her opening.

"Not too fast," she murmured. "I've seen that massive cock."

How many times had I heard that before…

"You can take it baby. I'll go easy on you."

She nodded and I eased in, the width of my cockhead stretching her to her limit. She winced and closed her eyes, taking deep and slow breaths. I paused, pulling back and moving my hips in micro strokes, letting her adjust.

"You okay?" I asked.

"More. I want more," she hummed after a moment, and I felt myself unknot even more inside.

I pushed my hips forward and watched as I disappeared into her glistening pussy. When my hips touched hers I almost cried, I was in such paradise. Never had such a pure, good woman taken me inside her.

I pistoned in and out, slowly at first, until she began to beg for more.

"God your cock is good, keep going. Keep fucking me," she murmured.

"Your pussy's tight baby, I'm gonna blow my load soon. Come now, baby, come on my cock."

Her muscles clenched and she shuddered, her head rocking from side to side on the bed as she came with a cry that triggered the explosion of my own orgasm. I gripped her legs in their vertical position and spread them open as if I might be able to drive myself deeper, and filled her with my cum, groaning through an exhausting finish.

She slumped into my arms when I lay beside her, shaking as I stroked her silky hair, thick pieces plastered to her neck and temples from perspiration. I ran my fingers over her breasts, admiring the flush on her chest from her deep orgasm.

We dozed off, time suspended as it does when you sleep.

Sometimes I wish things could just stay that way.

CHAPTER 18

JOELLE

"Hey, I gotta get up," Blaze whispered in my ear.

I started—for a split second I didn't know where I was, or why Blaze, the dude that hated me more than anything, was even speaking to me.

And then I remembered, and stretched my arms and legs, feeling like a million bucks. Well, except for my purple ankle. And I was a little sore *down there*.

I watched him pull on boxers and jeans, and then a tattered old rock concert T-shirt.

Did he have to leave?

"Why don't you slow down and get back in bed with me?" I teased, lowering the blankets to give him a nice view of my breasts.

He sat next to me on the bed, pulling on his socks and shoes. "I have a lot to do today," he said firmly.

Oh cripes. Was he going back to being a hard-ass

jerk? After he'd nearly fucked the stuffing out of me? I mean, didn't that count for something?

But I could hear it in his voice, and the twinkle in his eye confirmed it. Something had changed between us. Gruff? Sure. Hard? Definitely.

But not a jerk.

He got up and pulled on a heavy fleece.

"Hey, hey, hey," I said. "Just give me a couple minutes, okay?" I reached for him and pulled him to me.

He sighed and sat back down. "Okay." He reached to ruffle my hair, and I was glad there was at least a little tenderness between us. I could take the gruff and hard, but I needed some assurance as well.

"Are you going to tell me about the closet? I really would listen, and I need to know… for reasons."

He ran his hand over his bald head, his bulky arms reminding me of how effortlessly he'd picked me up the night before.

"I can't tell you much. At least not yet—"

"What? Why?" He was exasperating the hell out of me.

He took a deep, thoughtful breath. Finally, he was going to spill the deets.

"What I can tell you is that you can't leave now." He looked at me with a completely straight face.

I loved a guy with a sense of humor.

I gave him a little play smack on the arm. "Aren't you the little joker?" I plopped back on the bed, hands behind my head. My vacation hadn't turned out too badly, after all.

"Whew. I had a feeling this might happen. I'm not kidding. You can't leave Savage Mountain," he repeated.

He looked pretty serious. Actually very serious. Maybe that's because he was?

I bolted upright in bed. "I hope you are pulling my leg."

He just stared at me.

"Blaze, there is no way you can keep me here, or anywhere for that matter. People will be looking for me. My car is parked at the trailhead. Someone will wonder why it's been there so long. They will come looking," I repeated, trying to convince myself someone really would.

My heart pounded, thinking I'd just spent the night with the fucker. God, how stupid could I get. Yeah, he and all the other guys were hot, but now they were keeping me *prisoner*?

I thrust my chin out so he knew I wasn't afraid. "I'll leave when I'm ready to, and there's not a goddamn thing you can do about it. Fuck you and fuck the rest of your posse. I'll report you to the authorities, and they'll take you all away. Especially when they see that weird-ass arsenal and uniform stash you're hiding. I bet you're not supposed to have any of that."

I began to stand, but he pushed me right back down with one hand.

"Sit."

"My friends will be looking for me, I'm serious. You can't do this."

Regardless of my brave front, my resolve was weakening. Nothing I said had any effect on him, and I was beginning to get scared. Hell, who was I kidding? I *was* scared. And my voice was turning whiny, like a stupid little bitch.

Don't beg. Whatever you do, don't beg.

At least I could hang on to my dignity.

"You don't have to worry about your friends," he said, looking directly at me. "And I'm telling you this because you asked."

"Oh really? And what's that supposed to mean?" I asked, trying to sound tough, but failing miserably.

"They've been contacted. We got Pippa's info out of your phone and called her when we went to town yesterday."

They weren't hunting? Instead, they'd gone to town? And called my friend?

I clenched my fists. "You've got to be kidding—"

"We told her you'd had an accident, and that you were healing nicely at our cabin. She was very grateful we called her. We told her you'd be away for a while."

Fuck me, this is nuts. They sold it off to Pippa and she said okay? What the fuck?

"You have got to be kidding. You can't do that. I have a job to get back to—"

He got up and pulled a down vest over his fleece. "You won't need that job anymore. Pippa's letting them know you've resigned. We have everything here that you need."

"You are fucking kidding me!" I shouted. "You quit my fucking job for me?"

Don't you know, the tears started. Fuck. The last thing I wanted to do was cry in front of this brute.

"And we picked up your car. It's in a private garage now, with ours."

Terror washed over me. "You're going to... god, no...."

Blaze winced, seeing what I was insinuating.

"No. That's not our style. Jo, what you need to know is that keeping you up here with us is what is keeping you alive. Now that you know us—and know a little about us—your life is in grave danger. And, interestingly, your friend was very effusive in her thanks for keeping *you* 'safe'. Jo, why is she so concerned about your remaining 'safe'? You have a little secret of your own, don't you? You haven't been entirely honest, *yourself*, have you?"

Fuck. "It's none... none of your business," I stammered. "And you aren't keeping me here against my will."

I'd get away if it was the last thing I did, so help me.

He pulled up a chair and faced me.

"We all have our secrets, Jo. And I'm hoping that when you hear ours, you'll understand that you're not so much a prisoner as... well, one of us. After all, why would you want to leave, knowing that people are after you, wanting to kill you, for stealing drugs?"

CHAPTER 19

Pierce

Blaze strode powerfully out of the house, and Jo could be heard sobbing quietly in his room, where he'd left her. Jax, Reid, and I sat in the living room in agony, seriously hurting for our girl.

Shit, did I just say *our girl*? I was such a pussy.

But we knew we had to give her some time. She'd come to us when she was ready.

"She sounds pretty upset," Jax said, quietly strumming his guitar.

She sure did. Anyone would, after knowing what we'd done, and what Blaze no doubt had told her.

Reid stood, running his hand through his long beard. "I'm hungry. Anyone want soup?" He headed to the kitchen where he heated up the previous night's dinner. Leftovers were shit, but better than nothing.

I was worried. I didn't expect Jo to take it well that she was basically under house arrest. Not that we called it that. But we guys had thought hard about how to handle the situation, and in the end had agreed that the only way to keep her safe was to keep her close.

And then her friend spilled the beans about the drug heist. Jesus, why couldn't we have hooked up with a girl with a less checkered past? I didn't mean a choir girl, but... Jesus, a girl on the run from drug dealers?

But hey, who was I to talk? I wasn't exactly an angel.

Come to find out Jo's little 'camping trip' had been a hideout while the thugs who were after her had passed through Vegas. Pippa was part of the drama, too, and fled to L.A. for a few days until the heat was off, after she'd banged up her hand or something.

She figured they had better chances of evading their hunters if they went in separate directions.

Pretty ballsy if you ask me, but then I'd known there was something badass about Jo since the first time I saw her at the campsite. I just hadn't been able to put my finger on it.

Speaking of which, she finally passed through the living room with her crutch. I knew she eventually would, since the front door was the only way to get to the outhouse.

Note to self: next mountain hideout to have indoor plumbing. Even I hated having to go outside at night, although pissing in the great outdoors was one of those little joys that men got to experience.

"Hey," Jax said, setting aside his guitar.

I felt like someone had just punched me in the gut when I saw her. She looked defeated. And tired. Like we'd broken her spirit.

If we'd caused her any irreparable damage, I wouldn't be able to live with myself. If her spark was gone forever, well I didn't know what I'd do.

I wanted to comfort her, to hold her in my arms and tell her that it would be okay. That we weren't her jailers, but inviting her to be… something more. With me. With *us*.

I wanted to offer her everything in that moment.

"Hey," she said quietly, without her usual reserve of energy. She was wearing one of Blaze's sweatshirts, which was about ten sizes too big, and her blonde hair was a tangled mess. But the most striking thing was the light in her eyes. Or rather, the absence of it. My heart crumbled a little, and I again wanted to embrace her, tell her all would be okay.

But I couldn't do that.

I didn't *know* whether everything would be okay.

"Jo, do you think we could talk to you? The three of us guys?" I asked.

Jax and Reid looked at her hopefully. Yeah, she was that important to us.

She shrugged, dejected. "Yeah, sure. It's not like I'm going anywhere." She laughed hollowly.

"Your ankle's looking a little better," Reid said.

She took a seat and looked at the foot that she'd

propped up on the coffee table. "I guess. It's not as swollen as it was."

"Jo," I started, "first, I want to say that Blaze is not the most diplomatic person. I know he told you some things this morning that may not have made sense to you."

She looked at me blankly.

"First off, we know about you. We know your secret, and we know what you were running from. But don't worry, no one will find you up here. In fact, we know some people who may be able to take care of the men who are after you and your friend."

"What? How? You can't get them off my back. They don't give up," she said, hope rising and falling in a single utterance. "They never will."

"Wait," I said, holding up a hand. "Let me finish and then we'll take care of questions. I think maybe that's what you need, because I know Blaze. He just tends to drop shit in your lap and then go storming out the door."

She tilted her head, impatient.

"The day we asked you to stay in the closet for a bit, and to remain quiet, was a day when we were receiving money from someone who can't be known, someone Blaze and I used to work for. If his identity were to be revealed, well, he would take drastic measures that you don't want to be on the receiving end of."

She shook her head, shrugging again. "I'm not following you. But I sure would like to know what all those freaking guns were for."

She had a right to know.

"Blaze and I used to be private security contractors. Simply put, mercenaries. We worked with governments and other organizations to take care of some jobs that would have been illegal for them to carry out, or jobs they didn't want to touch with a ten-foot pole. Think about it. If there was something the government doesn't want to do, even with all those black ops outfits they have, you know it had to be pretty freaking bad."

I'd never discussed this with anyone except the guys in the house, and that had been a long time ago. Talking about my past out loud after all that time made my heart pound. It was the biological and physiological price of the work I once did. It had left invisible but lasting scars.

Confusion crossed her face. "And? What's with the guns, and why are you keeping me here?"

"We will be keeping low profiles for the rest of our lives. Fortunately, there are people who are helping make sure we stay off the grid and therefore remain safe. That was part of our agreement in going to work for them. Now that we're retired, certain... friends... look out for us and keep us happy. But that also means if they smell trouble, they take care of it."

Reid brought Jo a hot cup of tea, which she took with both hands.

"We didn't want anyone to know you were here, and since you've discovered what we're really all about, you're essentially one of us now," I added. "I'm not sure Blaze would feel comfortable if you left."

"What about Reid and Jax? You guys weren't mercenaries, were you?" she asked, looking between the two.

Jax shook his head no. "You know my reason for being here. Pierce picked me up and dusted me off after I lost my wife and daughter."

She turned to Reid, who nodded. "My dad went to prison for embezzlement. We lost the family business and everything, so I came up here," he said. "I've been rebuilding myself... my life."

"The island of misfit toys," she murmured.

She had that right.

"And now that we know you have some secrets of your own, all the more reason to stay with us," Jax added.

"And there is another reason we want you here, Jo," I said.

"What?" she asked.

I looked at the other guys. We'd discussed this, and it felt right to bring it up now.

"This is gonna sound so fucking stupid. But... we... we've grown attached to you, Jo. We care about you. A lot."

She put down her mug, her brows knit in concern. "You do?"

I nodded. "Yup. We want you here so you can get to know us better. And to find out how *you* feel about *us*. All four of us."

"You mean... "

"Yeah, Jo," Reid stumbled, "we... like you a lot."

"It would be nice if you stayed willingly, to see where things could go with us. All of us," I added.

"I don't get it. *All* of you? What does that mean?"

I finally felt like I was making progress expressing what was in my heart. What was in all our hearts.

"Will you give us a chance, Jo?" I asked.

CHAPTER 20

JOELLE

Wait, wait, wait.

I sat on the sofa, my gaze moving between Pierce, Jax, and Reid, while I held a cup of steaming tea close to my chest, as if it could protect me.

Of course, Blaze had bailed. While I'd initially thought he was the hard-hearted fucker of the group, I was figuring out his habit of withdrawing, and of being a prick, was his way of dealing with his intense sensitivity.

Who would have known? The biggest, baddest guy in the house was a kind and compassionate man. Hell, when we'd made love the night before, I could have sworn at one point there were tears in his eyes.

But that would remain our secret. I liked having something of him that was all mine.

Actually I felt that way about all the guys. They

were all so different from the other, and my time with each had been precious in completely different ways.

They wanted me to stay.

Actually, they were pretty much *making* me stay. But they also *wanted* me to.

How fucked up was that?

"I... I don't know what to say. It's all really confusing. There's a lot to digest, to think through. I mean, I have my own issues, then you guys have yours," I said slowly.

They wanted me to be with them. I didn't even know what that meant, and I wasn't sure how to ask.

"Can't believe you found out about the drugs," I said, shaking my head.

Reid came over and sat next to me, placing an around my shoulders. "Yeah. Before we called Pippa, we pretty much knew what was going on, anyway."

"What? How?" I asked.

Reid looked a tad embarrassed, and I pretty much knew what he was going to say. "We went through your stuff and had our contacts run a check on you. We knew you'd been arrested for the drug charge, and gotten off. It wasn't hard to figure out there would be some bad guys trying to track you down. And we were right."

Of course. They'd gone through my shit. Why was I not in the least bit surprised?

"I can't believe I got in trouble for snooping in your freaking weapons room, when you helped yourselves to my life," I grumbled. "You guys really are fucked up, you know that?"

"Guilty as charged," Pierce quipped. "We had to find out if you'd been hired to take us out or not. When you've been in a profession like Blaze and me, you learn to watch over your shoulder, all the time. Trust no one."

"But *me*? You thought *I* might have been a hit man? Or hit woman?"

Pierce shrugged. "Doesn't take a lot of strength to pull a trigger."

I'd truly landed in crazy town.

Jax leaned forward on his chair. "Care to tell us what happened with the drug heist?"

Oh. That.

I took a deep breath. Why the hell not? They knew everything else about me.

"Pippa and I were waitressing in Philadelphia. The bar manager was dealing pills and some other stuff, I was never sure what. I figured it was 'roids—he was one of those meathead motherfuckers who spent all his free time in the gym. But either way, he was a total ass. One night after closing, Pippa and I sneaked into his office and stole his stash. We just wanted to fuck with him. But somehow he figured it out, and apparently it was worse than roids. He set his henchmen loose on us, so we left town. He was also friends with a lot of cops. We were afraid he'd kill us."

Pierce was frowning. "What did you do with the drugs?"

Of course they were going to ask me that.

"We totally freaked out and dumped them in the fucking Delaware River," I admitted. "Lucky thing too, the cops picked us up about two hours later. When they had no evidence, they had to let us go. We were on the highway west before the sun rose."

Pierce looked at Reid, who looked at Jax.

Then they all burst out laughing.

Reid slapped his knee. "You guys are such badasses, stealing someone's drugs, and then you didn't know what the hell to do with them, so you chucked them in a river? Goddamn."

It was true. We hadn't known what to do with them.

Jax stopped laughing long enough to catch his breath. "And then you go to Vegas, of all cities?"

Lovely, having a laugh at my expense.

I shrugged. "We didn't know how to tell the guy we'd dumped his shit. But we have managed to keep at eye on the guy since then. So far, we've always managed to stay a couple steps ahead of him."

Pierce shook his head. "So much for your life of crime." He looked at the guys and they all started laughing again.

For some reason, I joined them. I felt good to laugh over what had kept Pippa and me on our toes for far too long, living in fear, and always looking over our shoulders. Although we weren't out of the woods yet.

"Pippa gave us the guy's name. We're having it looked in to," Pierce added. "We know a few people out that way."

"Wha… what does that mean?" I demanded.

"Don't worry about it, okay?" Pierce said.

Christ, these guys were hit men on top of all the other shit they'd told me?

"So, I guess all our secrets are out now," I said, looking at all of them. I stood. "Excuse me."

Holy shit. I hobbled out to the potty, happy for a moment to clear my head.

Mercenaries? Drugs? Me with four guys?

No more Maid to Order?

My head was spinning, and as I crutched back to the house, I nearly wiped out from not paying attention. Just what I needed—another injury.

As if there hadn't been enough surprises in the last twenty-four hours of my life, when I returned to the house, the three guys were standing in the living room, lined up like soldiers, hands folded right in front of their crotches.

I guess to hide their genitals. Because they were naked. Butt naked.

Like not a stitch of clothing on.

My legs felt really heavy, and I grabbed a chair to keep from crumbling.

On top of that, my mouth had gone dry. "Wha… what… are you doing?" I asked, trying not to stare at the three beautiful penises in front of me as the hands hiding them moved out of the way.

Pierce walked over and took my hand. "We're going to show you how we feel about you."

He brought me to the sofa, where three pairs of

giant hands lifted Blaze's huge sweatshirt over my head, leaving me standing just as naked as the guys were. For a split moment, I was embarrassed, but that quickly passed into a feeling of power.

I felt beautiful, desired by these incredible men who, really, had nothing but the best in mind for me since we'd met at my campsite and I'd made them coffee. Actually, since Jax had spied on my skinny dipping.

My little perv. I would get him back for that, some day.

I was surrounded by hundreds of pounds of hard muscle, my hands roaming every bit within my reach.

And their lips, so soft as they tasted my neck, shoulders, arms, and hands, it was as if I were floating. I couldn't feel myself touching the ground, and even my bad ankle stopped hurting. Every pore on my body was hyper-sensitized, screaming for caresses and stroking. I was starving and these men were the only thing that could save me.

Jax pushed me down onto the sofa, where he quickly got to work, his mouth on my pussy. Reid kneeled on the sofa next to me, and I took his length all the way down my throat, wanting to give him the same kind of pleasure I was feeling. And Pierce, my darling Pierce, stood with a smile, watching his friends work me over while he stroked himself.

"How do you feel, baby?" Reid asked, his face glistening from my pussy juices.

I smiled at him with half-closed eyes. "Mmmm…"

was all I could manage to say.

"Are you ready to be fucked?" Pierce asked, and I almost came right there. How did those guys know just what to say and do to get my motor revving?

Reid and Jax each took one of my legs while Pierce stretched a condom over his cock, and stood before me.

"I am ready. Please fuck me."

"Open yourself for me," he said, gesturing with his chin.

My hands wandered over my breasts, my stomach, and down to my pussy, where I slipped my fingers between my wet folds. Reid and Jax, holding my legs higher, and stroking themselves with their free hands, watching me touch myself with satisfied smiles.

"Look at the guys, baby. They like seeing you play with your pussy," Pierce breathed.

"Yeah? You guys like this, too?" I asked, and opened my lips so they could see my most intimate parts—my throbbing clit and opening, which was already leaking with my cum, so much so that it ran down my ass and onto the sofa beneath me.

Pierce got down on one knee and ran his thumb up and down my slit, easily accessible since I had opened myself to him. "That's right. Open yourself for us. Pull on those lips."

I parted my flesh and put two fingers inside myself to make way for Pierce. He slid into my opening, past my fingers, until he was up to his balls inside me.

That's when I stopped thinking. My mind went

blank. All I could do was feel, in my body, in my heart, and in my soul.

He plunged again and again inside me, pushing me back against the sofa, unable to move. I was held in place by the guys gripping my legs, who I in turn held on to. My head lolled back and forth as I shook, my breath coming in gasps until an orgasm thundered over me. I'm not sure if I screamed or was silent, because the blood rushing through my ears drowned out all sound and thought.

Everything was pleasure, pure pleasure.

My legs fell back into place. My senses returned. I snuggled into the arms of one of the guys, I wasn't sure which, but I felt wrapped in the warmth of everybody's care.

"Well, what do we have here?" Blaze chuckled from the doorway, where he stood with a big smile.

"Dude. Thought you'd never get here," Pierce said, stepping aside for his friend. "We've been... showing her the benefits of staying."

"I see," he said. "And?"

"And I'm going to stick around awhile," I answer, spreading my legs more. "If you can satisfy me."

Instead of answering, Blaze headed straight for me, and pulled me to my feet. Well, to my foot, to be more accurate.

And now that I had a better idea of where I fit in, I met his gaze head on.

His lips slammed into mine as the rest of the guys whistled approvingly.

CHAPTER 21

JAX

The next week flew by and Jo's ankle got stronger every day. In fact, she finally got to the point that if she were really careful she could put a little weight on it.

Guess the fresh air and sunshine—not to mention a bunch of great sex—could cure all kinds of ills.

We also spent time showing her our lives. I'd taken her into the woods to show her how to chop wood. It was really more of a demonstration, since she wasn't steady enough on both feet to handle an axe. But she was eager to learn a few of the skills needed to keep our little household running.

I loved that about her.

Shit, did I just say love? Guess so. Honestly, it felt nice.

"So what was your wife's name?" she asked at one

177

point, as we headed back to the cabin. She used a crutch under one arm, but I didn't need to support her anymore. I just pushed the cart of chopped wood alongside her, making sure she kept her balance.

Christ. I hadn't talked about the accident in so long. But that didn't mean I didn't think about it every day.

"Her name was Raffa."

"Pretty."

I nodded. "She was beautiful. Long hair, tawny skin, full lips. One of those natural sun goddess types. Our baby girl was going to look just like her when she grew up."

"How did it happen?"

My heart pounded. But I wanted to talk about it. I *needed* to talk about it. Especially with Jo.

I swallowed hard.

"I'm sorry," she said. "I shouldn't have asked."

"No, it's okay. I want you to know. And maybe I need to let it out some too."

She stopped and looked directly at me.

"I'd been out drinking with Pierce at our favorite bar. We'd been buddies for years, and I knew a little of his background, but didn't poke too deeply. I'd had a couple beers too many, so I called Raffa for a ride. She didn't want to come because she'd just put the baby down, but I pressured her because I didn't want to drive home. On the way to pick me up, they were hit by a truck, a semi whose driver thought he could beat the red light."

The color drained from Jo's face, and when she'd

composed herself, she put her hands on either side of my face, tilting her forehead to mine. "I'm so, so sorry."

I studied her beautiful face, covered in a light spray of freckles that added an air of innocence, which contradicted her true badass self.

"Yeah. They were there, and then they weren't. I was a husband and father, and then I wasn't. I knew what the rest of my life was going to look like, and then... I didn't."

She gulped, nestling into the crook of my neck, giving me her strength. "That's when Pierce brought you up here?"

"Yeah. He'd returned from several years abroad doing his 'private security' thing as he called it then, and his mom had passed in the meantime. The cabin had become his. Perfect timing, really. Reid and I agreed to Pierce and Blaze's security regimen, and the rest is history."

"Thank you for sharing your story with me," she said, stroking my face. "And thank you for... for accepting me."

We started walking again, and as we neared the house, it was my turn to stop.

I had something to get off my chest. "Jo, I want you here at the house. I... I've gotten attached to you in a way I never thought I would after I lost my wife. I know we're still getting to know each other, but my instincts are usually right about things. And I know the other guys feel the same way." I stared at her. I couldn't help myself.

She nodded, and then looked down at her feet. "I'm honored. But I don't see how I could choose one of you, and hurt the others. I just could never do that."

Her eyes filled with tears. Now I felt like shit for making her cry.

"I can't choose. I may have to stay here indefinitely, but I won't choose among you. I won't."

With that, she turned and hobbled the rest of the way to the house on her own.

I gave her some time, then went to her room.

"Jo?" I asked.

I heard sniffles. "Hey Jax. Come in."

She was lying back on Pierce's bed with her foot elevated.

"We're taking a trip into town, and we were wondering if you'd like to come. We make quick trips there every now and then, after one of our contacts combs the area for any potential trouble."

She sat straight up. "Wow. Are you serious? No way. I can get some personal things, as well as some fruits and veggies."

"All right. Cool. We'll leave in an hour. And I have one thing to add."

"Yeah?"

"Personally, I think it's your business if you leave. You know, in case you don't want to stay here with us. I'm sure that's part of the reason Blaze said something to me about the trip, to give you the choice. But Blaze is not exaggerating that your life will be in serious danger. The men Blaze and Pierce were involved with... they don't care about us, or you. They care about Blaze and Pierce staying quiet and out of the way. Just keep that in mind if you are inclined to go AWOL."

She was quiet on the trip to town, I figured because she was probably exhausted, or maybe disturbed by the story of my wife and child. To get to our truck, and then into town, you have to hike two miles, and then it's a long drive down the mountain.

But I know she was also thinking through what we'd talked about—whether she wanted to be with any of us guys.

But we weren't going to pressure her. She needed time. We respected that.

Besides, it wasn't like we were going anywhere.

We pulled into the tiny town where we always ran our errands. "All right, Jo. There's the variety store. You can get all sorts of girlie shit in there," Blaze said in his typical gruff way. "Pierce and I have to go to the bank, and Reid and Jax will do the grocery shopping. Meet back here at the truck in forty-five minutes."

Jo hobbled off to the store, and Blaze and Pierce disappeared to do their thing, leaving Reid and me.

"How is she doing, Jax? Can you tell?" he asked.

I pursed my lips. I knew what he was asking... was she going to stay, or walk? "Not sure. She mentioned feeling like she has to choose one of us guys. I guess I wouldn't want to be in her position."

Reid shrugged as we neared the grocery store. He knew the truth, and knew it was just taking a little longer to soak into Jo's head. "But she doesn't have to choose."

"I know. Give her time. She'll figure it out," I said.

He turned around and watched her walk slowly into the store. "How do we know she won't disappear?"

"We've done our best. I'm shocked Blaze has been as open with her as he's been, explaining all he has. If she takes off in spite of that, then that's on her."

Reid frowned. "Yeah, fine, it's dangerous for her, but what about us? She knows about us. How do we know that in her effort to bail on us, she won't lead the wrong people right to us?"

"That's exactly why I think she won't leave. She cares about us now."

"I hope you're right," Reid said.

CHAPTER 22

JOELLE

Back to civilization.
      Stores. Phones. Electricity.
Flush toilets.

Hair conditioner.

I would never again take any of those things for granted.

I flipped through the clothing racks of a dumpy little store called, of course, Savage Mountain Mercantile. I mean, it wasn't horrible, and it probably served the needs of the town perfectly well, but how many plaid flannel shirts and Wrangler jeans can a girl have?

I sniffed around for some cute yoga pants and a strappy tank top or two, but no go. So I picked up a few T-shirts, *Hanes Beefy-T's* to be exact, figuring that when I got back to the cabin I could be creative with some scissors and a needle and thread.

Cripes, I sounded like a real frontier woman or something. Next trip, I'd be buying a bolt of cloth and sewing a new wardrobe for everyone.

Ditto with the footwear. I wouldn't have minded something sturdy and cute, but they had cowboy and hiking boots, and that was about it. I saw a pair of Birkenstock sandals in a sale bin and snapped them up.

I'd never liked those sorts of shapeless, unisex shoes, but I didn't have much choice just then, did I?

In addition to the clothes, I grabbed all the toiletries I thought I might ever need, and I paid for everything out of the five hundred dollars cash Blaze had given me. I'd hoped for some sexy undies and maybe a bra or two, but all they'd had were three packs of nasty cotton granny panties.

Yeah, no.

I had no idea how long I'd be staying at the cabin with the guys, but I planned to keep my time there as fun—and sexy—as possible.

Speaking of which, the guys were into me, and I was into them. A grinding confusion wore on me, where I felt I needed to make a decision I knew I could not, because I wanted them all, and I wanted them equally.

That was fine if we were all fucking around, but what about long term? When feelings got heavy, and things got serious-serious, like I could already tell was happening with Jax, what happened then?

There was no way things were going to end well. People would be hurt, hearts would be broken, and I'd be up shit's creek, because that's always how things always turned out for me. I really, really needed to talk to Pippa, but the guys had told me it was dangerous to use my cell phone.

Which sucked balls.

With twenty minutes to kill, and the guys nowhere in sight, I decided to pop into the ice cream shop a couple doors down. The guys had told me not to stray off the main street, and to keep my head down, but shit, nobody there knew me.

I was sure a little ice cream cone would be fine.

So, loaded down with my new purchases and two scoops of strawberry on a sugar cone, I returned to the truck, taking a seat on the curb next to it while I waited for the guys to return.

It seemed like a cute little town, eons away from the craziness I was used to in Vegas. There were old timers walking down the street hand in hand, and a small gaggle of kids rushing to buy something to eat and get back to school.

A simple life. Not as simple as at the cabin, without its electricity and indoor plumbing, but simple.

But was it for me? I wasn't so sure.

I *was* sure, however, of my feelings for the guys. And those feelings had me worried. The thought of trying to choose one almost took the pleasure out of the ice cream I was enjoying on the curb in the sunshine, with my shopping. Almost.

Well, at least the drug-dealer ex-boss and his henchmen would never find me.

Someone tapped me on the shoulder, startling me so badly that my ice cream fell right off my cone and onto the ground in front of me. All I was left with was the cone in my hand, and sticky pink stuff running down my fingers.

Goddamnit. That ice cream was good.

I peered up and over my shoulder. Who the hell had scared me like that?

"Oh, sorry ma'am. Didn't want to make you lose your ice cream. Let me buy you another one," a nondescript woman with curly brown hair said, peering down at me.

I looked at the ice cream on the pavement, now full of dirt, melting into rivulets.

"That's okay. I'd had enough anyway. You know, waistline and all."

The woman stood there, just out of my line of sight while I tried to mop myself up with the sole napkin I had.

"Is there something I can do for you?" I asked her.

"Jo?" a male voice said behind me.

That time, I dropped everything and jumped to my feet. And the male voice that had said my name?

It wasn't one of the guys from the cabin.

I was on my feet and my heart was pounding. Normally, a stranger approaching me would barely give me any pause, even if they knew my name. I would have just thought it was someone I'd met once and forgotten. But it seemed Blaze and the others had really struck some fear in me. Which was their intention. I'd thought they were exaggerating, but the way the hairs stood on the back of my neck, I was beginning to think they were right to warn me.

I squared my shoulders and tried to look tough. "Who are you?" I asked a rough-looking dude in sunglasses. The woman who'd tapped me was hustling down the sidewalk almost at a run. She glanced back over her shoulder, whipped around a corner, and was gone.

Something was terribly off.

I observed this while the guy before me smiled, showing nasty yellow teeth, and deep creases in his leathery skin.

"Don't worry about who I am, Jo. You're coming with me." Before I could move, he had a death grip on my arm.

"Get off me," I shouted as loudly as I could.

It was one of the tricks I'd learned at the restaurant when someone was harassing me. The bouncer would be over in seconds and the offending diner would be out on his ass. It also worked in the Vegas streets, where people would normally intervene in that situation.

Only this time, there was no bouncer.

But there were my mountain men.

CHAPTER 23

REID

"Cripes, we got a lot of fruit. I hope it doesn't go bad before we eat it all. You know I hate wasting food," I said as Jax and I hustled back to the truck. To be honest, I was getting a little nervous about Jo being off on her own.

That and I didn't know what a *mangosteen* was. When did the little town grocery get all that hippie bullshit?

Jax shifted the four overloaded grocery bags he was carrying in his arms. "Relax, would you? Jo says she likes fresh food, and she's right that we don't get enough of it up at the cabin."

"So we're gonna front load on the veggies for the next two weeks, and then have none until we get back down here?"

Jax rolled his eyes. "Maybe you can take up canning, bro. You need something to do with all your free time."

"Dude, you should talk. Maybe you can start a vegetable garden or something with your free time? You're the one always playing your guitar."

"Yeah? Well you're the one always rubbing one out —" he said.

I stopped short. "Holy fuck. Is that Jo up there, by the truck?" Some dude was pulling on her arm. She was trying to fight him off unsuccessfully, but giving him hell in the meantime.

"Shit," Jax said, dropping his groceries and breaking into a run.

He sprinted down the street, with me on his heels.

The guy saw us coming for him, and reached into the back of his jeans, a gun appearing in his right hand. Just as he was aiming it at us, Jo fell, the guy's hand still clamped on her arm. It jerked his other hand up, and the round flew harmlessly into the air.

What the fuck?

Jo yanked her arm free, and she struck, uppercutting the guy in the balls even as he tried to turn his pistol on her. A second later, Jax was all over the guy, hitting him like a linebacker.

Running full speed, Jax had slammed him into the brick wall behind him. The gun had clattered to the ground and to her credit, Jo had scooped it up. By the time I reached them, Jax had slammed the guy to the concrete, and was well on his way to knocking him out.

"Jax, Jax, wait. We need to question him." I pushed Jax out of the way, and yanked the semi-conscious man up, getting into his bloody face.

"Who are you? Who sent you?" I asked as blood poured from his nose and he mumbled, his eyes rolling up.

Jax, not happy with his takedown of the guy, kicked him in the ribs for good measure. "Fucking asshole. What were you doing to her?"

"Guys." Blaze's voice came from behind. "Zip tie his hands and feet and load him into the truck."

We only had moments, not wanting to garner unwanted attention, but Pierce and Blaze were experts at what they were doing. As we threw him in the back of the truck, I checked the guy's pockets. They were empty, obviously on purpose.

"No identification," I said.

Everything had happened so fast, I'd lost sight of Jo. But I was happy to see she was in Pierce's arms, holding on to him for dear life.

"Okay, gang," Blaze said. "Let's load up our stuff and get the hell out of here before someone gets nosy."

I rode in the back of the pickup with our captive, sitting on his thighs to keep him from rolling around on the truck bed, particularly when Jax took a turn too fast. The guy probably already had a concussion, but I was sure Blaze wouldn't want him dead... yet.

When we were about twenty miles out of town, we pulled down an overgrown dirt lane until we could no longer be seen from the road.

Blaze pulled him out of the truck and threw him to the ground where he thrashed and moaned.

"Wake up, asshole," he said.

"Ohhh…" he moaned, wailing in self pity. "You broke my nose… "

Jax kicked him in the same spot he had before. If the man didn't already have broken ribs, I bet he did now.

"Who hired you?"

"Fuck you."

Blaze pulled out the gun Jo had picked up from the sidewalk, pointing it at his head. "Five seconds. Who hired you?"

Blaze's eyes quickly convinced the man what was up.

"I don't know who hired me. Some PI from the East Coast wired me money and gave me the bitch's picture. Told me to bring her to Vegas while I find the other girl."

Holy shit. Fucking Philly… just had to be.

"What's your name, shitbrain?" Blaze asked.

"J… John."

"Yeah, I bet your name is John," Blaze scoffed. "Look. We're gonna let you live. But we're leaving you here, in the middle of nowhere. Town's about twenty miles down the hill. You get lucky, someone might come by and give you a ride. Either way, will you take a message back to your bosses, John?"

Jax was holding him by the hair on his head, and helped him nod *yes*.

"You may think you know who Jo is, but you have no idea who we four guys are. And if they know what's good for them, they won't try to find out. It won't end well for them, or any of their associates. We know a lot of people and have a lot of friends. We can make things happen. Will you pass that on?"

"Yeah… yeah, I will," he sputtered, the stream of blood under his nose starting to congeal.

"As for you… I suggest finding a new line of work. Now. Somewhere in Mexico, maybe. Because if we see you on our mountain again, you're going to be fertilizer," Pierce interjected, cutting the man's bonds.

"Now go."

We jumped back in the truck and continued toward the cabin, leaving Jo's assailant twenty miles from anywhere. He'd find his way back, but it would be a long, painful trip.

"You all right, Jo?" I asked, pulling her to me in the backseat.

"I think so. Thank you. All of you," she said quietly.

"I'm sorry you had to go through that, but I'm glad Reid and Jax happened along at the right time," Pierce said.

"You guys should have seen the fight she was putting up. I'm not sure she really needed any of us," I said, laughing. "I mean, you uppercut the guy in the balls. I haven't seen that since Monday night wrestling as a kid."

That got a smile out of her. "Ya know, if any of you guys ever need a bodyguard, I'm available."

Laughter rolled through the truck.

"When your ankle is healed, Jo, I'd like to teach you some real moves. And to shoot, as well," Pierce said.

She snuggled into me tighter, the reality of her new life having taken hold. "Um. Okay. I guess so."

Pierce turned from the front seat to face Jo. "Hey, since we're all together, we wanted to discuss something with you, Jo."

She perked up and looked around the truck.

"What? What's up?" she asked, looking at each of us in turn.

He continued. "We know you've felt some pressure to choose among us. You know, to pick one of us to be your guy."

She looked down at her hands. "I know. I've wanted to discuss this with all of you, too. What I wanted to say is—"

"Wait. Please Jo, first listen to what we have to say," he said.

I reached for one hand, and Jax grabbed the other.

"What we want to say, Jo," Pierce said, hesitating for a moment, "is that we want you to be with all of us. You don't have to choose one over the other."

She gripped my fingers tightly. "What? What do you mean?"

"We mean, you don't have to choose," Blaze said, turning off the main road onto the single-lane one that lead to the cabin. We still had fifty miles or so to go. "You can have all of us. We would all be your companions. We'd all be your lovers. If you'll have us."

She released my hand, and hers flew up to her mouth. She squeezed her eyes shut, despite the tears that managed to seep out. I was glad she was getting emotional. That told me she cared. I glanced over at Jax, who nodded lightly at me.

Before we'd made the trip to town, the guys and I had discussed what we each wanted, and what we thought would be best for Jo. However, in the end, it was her decision to make. I knew what I hoped for, but whichever way she went was fine with me. For all the guys, our top priority was her happiness.

"Oh my god, you all are so wonderful. You've done so much for me. Saved my life, really. Oh shit. And now I'm crying," she said with a laugh.

"You don't have to give us your answer now. And we'll respect whatever you decide. If this doesn't work for you, it doesn't work for any of us," Pierce added.

"No, I think I can give you an answer."

I don't know about Blaze, Pierce, or Jax, but I held my breath.

C'mon girl, don't let us down…

"I accept your offer. I love you. All of you."

CHAPTER 24

JOELLE

As one might imagine, that was a festive night at the cabin.

We poured some excellent wine that had been saved for a special occasion, and Blaze put on his usual amazing spread. With the fresh fruit we managed to rescue from the street, I pulled together a cobbler that was so delicious, there wasn't a crumb of it left.

Those guys had some seriously big appetites.

After we'd cleaned up—they wouldn't let me lift a finger because they didn't want me thinking they wanted me around just to be their maid—I took them all into my bedroom, which by now Pierce had pretty much moved out of. He said I deserved a room of my own, for which I was very grateful.

I figured soon enough they'd build some sort of

extension to the cabin. Hopefully a real bathroom was on the list.

The guys watched me as I slowly undressed, one piece of clothing at a time. When I was down to my lacy thong, I turned and bent to step out of it, and heard a couple sexy groans behind me. I wanted to get the boys' engines revved, and give them a night to remember.

I started with Pierce, my first lover in the group, and the one who brought me into the family. I pushed his blond hair off his face, and kissed his temples while I unbuttoned his jeans from my position on the edge of the bed. He puts his hands on his hips, observing to see what I might do.

The other guys watched and squirmed, probably wondering about their turns.

Patience my loves, patience.

I pull Pierce into my mouth, and he dropped his head back and moaned. I sucked him hard, letting him hit the back of my throat, swallowing the urge to gag.

A low hum erupted from his throat, turning into a gritty moan.

"Fuck baby, suck me like that… oh fuck!" he bellowed, and spurted his hot cum into my mouth.

When he was done ejaculating, I slowly let him slip out of my mouth, his cock still hard. I wanted to clean every last drop off him, and I did.

Reid, who had initially be so opposed to my being at the cabin, stood with his cock in his hand already, smiling while he gazed at me. The look could only be described at love.

"C'mon over here, darlin'," I said. "How do you want me?"

"Jax, hand me a condom, will you," he said, gesturing to the nightstand. "And you, lay back."

As soon as I did, Reid's tongue was lapping me from clit to ass. There wasn't an inch that he missed. Then he lay back on the bed, and pulled me on top.

He held his cock for me to take at my own pace, watching as I lowered myself. As he disappeared inside me, I relished the sensation of his filling my pussy.

I fucked him slowly at first, then furiously, bouncing on him while he pulled and twisted my nipples. He threw his head back on the bed, squeezed his eyes shut, and groaned as he exploded inside me. I plastered my mouth to his to increase our connection, and my own orgasm hit me like a truck.

He held me as I shuddered, my head bucking back and forth.

I climbed off Reid, taking a sip of the water Jax had handed me.

"Lay back," he demanded, propping my legs over his shoulders.

At the same time, Blaze moved toward me on the bed, fisting himself as he aimed for my mouth. I opened eagerly, wanting to taste him. I heard Jax roll out a condom and he notched himself at my opening.

Grabbing the sheets for purchase, I sucked Blaze as deeply as I could while I waited to feel Jax inside me.

"Blaze," Jax said in a low growl, "do you think she's ready for me?"

Blaze chuckled, a twinkle in his eye. "Hmmm. Not sure. Give her a try." He thrust his hips to get deeper in my mouth, and I nodded my approval.

Jax entered me to his balls in one swift motion, dipping in and out as Pierce took my legs and held them straight up in the air. Closing them as he did tightened my pussy, and Jax released a shout of satisfaction that would have scared off a momma bear.

"It's my turn with your pretty pussy, isn't is baby," he said, watching my cheeks hollow as Blaze's cock disappeared in and out of my mouth.

I nodded as best I could and reached to pull myself open for him. He looked down and smiled.

"Such a pretty pussy," he growled, pounding me over and over.

Faster, harder, I imagined saying as the two guys pummeled me.

Another orgasm thundered over me and Blaze exploded in my mouth, pulling out in time to come on my tits. I gasped, grateful for the air, as I rubbed his warn cum into my skin.

"Oh, fuck!" Jax bellowed, coming while driving into me so hard I felt like I might break in two. "Goddamn," he murmured as he emptied himself in me.

"Wow," I murmured, forcing my eyes open to see my lovers all standing above me, watching and caring for me.

Reid left and returned to the room with a warm washcloth and started rubbing me down, cleaning me, as Blaze stroked my hair, and Pierce held my hand. Jax climbed into the bed next to me and eased the covers up as I dozed off in his arms.

BLAZE

Y eah, I was the dick in the group. I was grouchy, unfriendly, and temperamental.

But my friends knew I'd do anything for them, including putting my life on the line. I guess that's why they put up with me. And now Jo seemed to be putting up with me too.

After I'd been so awful to her when she'd first arrived, I quickly fell in love with her. Maybe that's why I was so difficult in the beginning—I sensed that change was afoot, and I was scared that my comfortable status quo was no longer going to exist.

I'd been through a lot in my mercenary work, and now that I was retired, I liked things predictable. I liked things in their place. I liked things *just so*.

But that approach to life wasn't sustainable. There

was too much to miss by not being open to new things. Like love.

And like making changes to the cabin.

I'd always told Pierce it was fine, rustic as it was. And it did function perfectly for four single guys. But when Jo came one the scene, it was obvious it was time for some upgrades, starting with indoor plumbing. It promised to be a big project, but doable, as we added a beautiful bathroom complete with a sauna and spa onto the side of the house, along with another bedroom.

We also expanded the solar panels, giving us more to work with than just a few LEDs outside the computer bank. It wasn't high luxury, but it was an upgrade.

Jo was especially happy with the home improvements. You can't expect a woman to be indefinitely happy with an outhouse.

Speaking of our girl, she had always been beautiful by any measure, but weeks in the woods had given her a healthy glow and joyousness I'd not seen when she'd first arrived. Her ankle healed well, and she regularly joined the guys in chopping wood, and even hunting when it was time to go out and get more meat. As sensitive as she was, she only shot at wild turkeys, and rarely hit one anyway.

But it was good that she was learning.

The week prior, she'd been up on the roof with one of us, cleaning out the gutters, showing us she could pull her weight. She did more than that, and was becoming special in every way.

She and I cooked together most nights. It was our special time together.

She and Jax played their music for us in the evening before one or more of us bedded her, depending on what folks were in the mood for. As threats against us diminished over time, we made plans. We weren't going anywhere yet, but there were people in L.A. who were interested in the music she wrote, and she couldn't wait to visit there.

Of course, Disneyland was on the agenda. I could even imagine myself wearing a pair of Mickey Mouse ears on my bald head.

Her ex-boss in Philly? Let's just say, he won't be bothering anyone again. Ever.

As Jo found her place in our lives, we found ours in hers. She quickly became the mistress of her home, and had an equal vote in our happy little world. She was a great balance to the abundance of testosterone that had once ruled the roost.

Yeah, she had us wrapped around her little finger. 'Course she was wrapped around ours, too.

That's the way it goes when you take up for someone else. You become family.

We didn't have it all figured out. But we loved our girl, and she loved us.

The rest would come.

EPILOGUE

I used to think I was kind of badass, the way I could carry heavy trays of shitty food around Maid to Order, that cheesy Vegas restaurant where I worked for so long. But then I never dreamed I'd someday be chopping down trees.

Yeah, me. I can chop down a tree. Now that was some badass shit.

The guys were doing all they could to leach the city out of me and make me a real mountain girl. I mean, I walked around now with a damn knife hanging off my belt. It had its own little leather pouch just like a trapper from the 1800s.

They also taught me archery, my favorite new hobby. They got me a custom-made bow—nothing fancy, just the traditional kind—but I practiced until my fingers were raw, and eventually, I could shoot better than any of them. They told me I'd soon be able to outshoot Katniss from The Hunger Games.

Renovations on the cabin were underway, which thrilled me to no end. We'd soon have a bathroom—like, a real bathroom, not the smelly, spider-infested outhouse kind. It was a big project that involved a lot of digging for a septic something or other, which was definitely not in my wheelhouse. So, I stayed out of the way and did my best to offer moral support. Oral support too, if you know what I mean.

I don't know what it was about being up on Savage Mountain, but my creativity had become unstoppable. Maybe it was the fresh air, but I suspect it was also from all the freaky sex I was having. It was like a dam had broken. There was this unstoppable flow of music pouring out of my pencil and onto my paper faster than I could get it down. Time would tell whether my songs were any good or not, although Jax seemed to think so when he played them on his guitar. But it felt amazing to be productive. Having that messed up ankle and looking over my shoulder in fear of the druggie guys for so long had seriously messed with my mojo.

Speaking of druggie guys, I never did find out exactly how or why they decided to leave Pippa and me alone. There was no doubt in my mind that my guys had something to do with the disappearance, but all they'd tell me was they'd made a couple calls, and that even they didn't know exactly how things had gone down. They'd hired someone who'd hired someone—something like that. Who knew that's how things in their crazy world worked?

One of those things that's better not knowing.

And, my girl Pippa. I was really missing her. When she finally got her butt up to Savage Mountain, I planned to take her straight to the pretty little campsite where it all started. Maybe we'd even stay for a couple days and camp, like real outdoors women. I'd finally convince her to quit that horrible Maid to Order place and come visit for a while so she could get to know Pierce, Jack, Reid, and Blaze, and get a taste of my new life. To further sweeten the pot, I told the guys had some buddies to introduce her to.

'Course now she wants her own harem.

Just like me.

DID YOU LIKE *The Captive*?

Check out *THE RUNAWAY*
and...
find all Mika Lane books here

GET A FREE SHORT STORY
Join my Insider Group
Exclusive access to private release specials, giveaways, the opportunity to receive advance reader copies (ARCs), and other random musings.

Dear Reader:

Please join my Insider Group and be the first to hear about giveaways, sales, pre-orders, ARCs, and most importantly, a free sexy short story: http://mikalane.com/join-mailing-list/.

Writing has been a passion of mine since, well, forever (my first book was "The Day I Ate the Milkyway," a true fourth-grade masterpiece). These days, steamy romance, both dark and funny, gives purpose to my days and nights as I create worlds and characters who defy the imagination. I live in magical Northern California with my own handsome alpha dude, sometimes known as Mr. Mika Lane, and an evil cat named Bill. These two males also defy my imagination from time to time.

A lover of shiny things, I've been known to try to new recipes on unsuspecting friends, find hiding places so I can read undisturbed, and spend my last dollar on a plane ticket somewhere.

I have several books for you to choose from including perennially favorite Billionaire and Reverse Harem romances. And have you see my Player Series about male escorts who make the ladies of Hollywood curl their toes and forget their names? Hottttt.... And my Anti-hero/Mafia books are now out in audio.

Check out my latest series, The Men at Work Collection, about hot men and the professions that make them successful masters of the universe... and the women they love.

I'll always promise you a hot, sexy romp with kick-ass but imperfect heroines, and some version of a modern-day happily ever after.

I LOVE to hear from readers when I'm not dreaming up naughty tales to share. Join my Insider Group so we can get to know each other better http://mikalane.com/join-mailing-list, or contact me here: https://mikalane.com/contact.

xoxo

Love,

Mika

Printed in Great Britain
by Amazon

87410385R00122